Richard Doddridge Blackmore

Christowell - A Dartmoor Tale

Vol. II

Richard Doddridge Blackmore

Christowell - A Dartmoor Tale
Vol. II

ISBN/EAN: 9783337024321

Printed in Europe, USA, Canada, Australia, Japan

Cover: Foto ©Andreas Hilbeck / pixelio.de

More available books at **www.hansebooks.com**

A Dartmoor Tale.

BY

R.^d Dr BLACKMORE,

AUTHOR OF "MARY ANERLEY," ETC.

"Splendidè mendax."

IN THREE VOLUMES.
VOL. II.

LONDON:
SAMPSON LOW, MARSTON, SEARLE & RIVINGTON,
CROWN BUILDINGS, 188, FLEET STREET.

1882.

LONDON:
PRINTED BY WILLIAM CLOWES AND SONS, LIMITED,
STAMFORD STREET AND CHARING CROSS.

CONTENTS OF VOL. II.

CHRISTOWELL.

CHAPTER I

AMONG THE JACKDAWS.

AMONG the good people of Dartmoor, very few subjects (outside of their own parish) arouse more interest, or create more wonder, than a town in the south-east of England, which used in plain days to be called London, but has no idea of being now described, except as " this mighty Babylon," or " our immense metropolis."

A man came down from London once to Christowell, by some accident, and he put up at the *Three Horse-shoes*, and he called for hot brandy and water. With wonderful speed, considering the size of the village, it was heard that he was there ; and nobody, who could help it, failed to go and see, what he was like. No idle curiosity was in their bosoms, neither any anxiety to drink his health—fearfully though he must require it, for every one had heard of the plague of London—but it was the clear wish of a large community, to recognize an envoy from one even larger. The gentleman, whose residence was in Whitechapel, could by no means understand their speech; but by help of a smoky old map in the bar—a better map than any that has been made since—he managed to try to get into their heads, by a bold exaggeration of his own, that London town was bigger than all Dartmoor. Now John Sage came in, before that was got over; and when he began to understand it—for his mind was slow, from its magnitude—the simplest truism from his lips made the bagman order slippers. For John said nothing rude, but stretched his arms across the hills, and valleys, of the map (which looked more vast from the fog shed over them by much smoke), and without turning round, he reflected thus: "Never wur I one of they, as goeth again' the Lor' Amaighty. Every day, a' doeth winders. But niver, if so be a' worked all Zinday, could a' create rogues enow, to orkapy all thiccy."

Perhaps this view of the matter is unsound;

though John was never contradicted, after he once turned fifty; for his father was known to have foretold, as true as a cathedral clock, the day of his departure from this world. But it may be argued, very soundly, that if there be, in London, lawyers honest; *a fortiori*, there must be other people of that same cumbrous quality. And, without any hazardous admission about that, it is enough to say, that in 1840, there might have been found, in the very heart of London, a firm of solicitors as honest as the day.

Messrs. Latimer & Emblin, of No. 10, Jackdaw's Court, Gray's Inn, had been in practice (through their ancestors, or selves), for upwards of a century; and their practice was quiet, and wise, and solid. With litigation they dealt so little, that if any one asked them who was the present Attorney-General, they went to the legal almanac to look, and after much consultation, sometimes put the saddle upon the wrong animal. Yet, being always accurate in the end, and very particular not to mislead, whenever they made a mistake, they always corrected it by post, at a nominal charge. And if, while alive, any lawyer can conciliate affection, it is by acknowledging that he was wrong; with a lenient charge for confessing it.

Even as the loftiest of all watch-makers—
"horologists" now they call themselves—will
not allow time to make any noise near him,
but glances in his office at a mute chronometer:
so the very deepest lawyers hush the clack of
law, on their own premises. It must be present
in the air; as the smell of cheeses from the
warehouse is, where only plugs are kept to
taste; but unless anybody asks too much, it
may try to pass for a sweet-smelling savour;
and to analyse such things, is seldom wise.

But though they declined all common-law
cases (except for some client of generations),
and had little to do with equity, these two
gentlemen were sound lawyers, and never gave
ill-advised advice. They would go through
the form of consulting counsel; as a solicitor
often does, when he knows much more than
the barrister, or at any rate works his knowledge better. But in reality, they relied upon
their own long experience, caution, good sense,
and the traditions of the firm. And whenever
they made a mistake, it was through undue
veneration for the latter. And such a mistake
they were making, at this time.

Mr. Latimer now was a venerable man,
wealthy, contented, and well-endowed with

those gifts of bygone generations—thick, snowy curls, and sound natural teeth. He was very particular about his dress, already becoming antiquated—that is to say, fine kersey breeches, black stockings, and buckled shoes, a straight-cut coat, a shirt, with a frill of the purest white cambric, (fastened with a brooch, containing a lock of his late wife's hair), and a roll-collar waistcoat of black silk; under whose margin, and upon a fair rotundity, glistened a broad watered ribbon, supporting a weighty gold ring of magnificent gold seals. With all these things his grave mild face, and dignified air comported well; making it difficult to imagine, and quite impossible to find, a more perfect specimen of a gentleman of business.

Mr. Emblin was nearly a score of years younger, taller by a head, and sparely framed. He had a little turn for sporting dress, but checked it, as much as he could, at the Office. He had some fine ideas of " going ahead," and lamented, at home, that his senior so sternly refused to have anything to do with a branch of business, now bringing in money by the bagful—to wit, the mighty schemes of mad railway companies. But he had a prudent wife, who told him of the ancient legend of

the bird in hand; also he had a shrewd head
of his own, and traditions of an ancestor who
had been ruined by the "South Sea bubble."
So that he managed to abstain; though it irked
him sadly, to see the ungodly (in the form of
inferior attorneys) puffed up with company
fatness, and swelling about, as if the round
earth was their rail.

This firm had large premises all their own;
for Jackdaw's Court belonged, only in part, to
the learned and honourable. Society. Sundry
people, sometimes so illegal as to be downright
costermongers, held their local habitation there,
by some original frankpledge; and if they were
questioned about their title, they supposed it
to be chaff, and made answer generally, that
they never stuck up to be nobs. But No. 10
stood apart from any contact with such
squatters, being a goodly house, rebuilt in the
reign of Queen Anne, as the date declared,
with Righteousness and Peace, above the third
floor windows, kissing each other in compo.

Now Righteousness and Peace, with a wreath
around them, relieved their airy costume with
black, and their rippling tresses with a wealth
of soot—at a shilling a bushel, which is fair
price—also the railings would have paid for

scraping, by a man who knows how to "utilize"; and many other little specks might have been discovered, by the boy who washed the windows of the Moreton folk. Still, when a gentleman once got in, he had many grounds for satisfaction, and perhaps for gratitude. For he found a good mat for his boots, and some landscapes to look at (instead of land, drawn and quartered, with arrows stuck through its disembowelment), also chairs of illegal nature, because they could give as well as take, and a power of attorney to sit down, and poke the fire, without prejudice.

On the first floor, a very tidy room contained some handsome old furniture, and the members of the firm, from ten until four o'clock of the day. No one, in those brave times, required sherry and sandwiches, or stout and oysters, at the witching hour of the legal noon, when writs are running rapidest, and clients go to and fro, most prone to be devoured; but the wiser manner of solid lawyers was, to dine at half-past five, with the hungry bosoms of their family around, and a quiet rubber, or sweet nap, in prospect. Though the railways already were beginning to screech out, to make the day hideous, and the night a nightmare.

Now a good drizzle often makes a fine day of business in London, because it is so dirty. If our "vast metropolis" attempted to be clean, it would never do half the trade it does. Not only because of the energy wasted in so vain an enterprise, nor even through the violence offered thus to nature; but chiefly because the people, coming with the money, would be in several minds about a bargain. When all is serene, and a walk, or drive, a pleasure, as in most continental cities, a customer (even though he be of British race) hangs over his cash more dubiously. "I can come again to-morrow; I will think about it; I will look into my bank-book, and perhaps consult my wife," is the unsatisfactory process of his mind; and the likelihood is, that he never comes again. But upon a day of good substantial dirt, with the drip of a myriad umbrellas in his neck, and a very safe note of bronchitis in his throat, his dogged resolution says, "Now, or never. I have ploughed through all this muck; and I mean business."

On that day, when the rain rushed down so savagely on Dartmoor, there was in London nothing more than a drizzle, bedewing the growth of business. Dirt came up between

the flag-stones, as if there were a crop of
cress to lift it; and getting kicked away by
scambling feet, slipped into a coat of slimy
mud. Impatient men, whose time was money,
at every advance lost twenty-five per cent.;
while the slow, knock-kneed fellow, from the
country, accustomed to slippery fallows, grinned.
And, though the neighbourhood of Gray's Inn
is not so very bad, when considered calmly,
backsliding occurred there, not only of hams,
but also of tongues under very learned wigs.

"It seems that we may almost go," said
Mr. Latimer, whose manner was to offer everything in *semble*; "it is getting rather dark, at
a quarter to four, even in what might be called
a summer month; or at any rate used to be so
considered. The extraordinary increase in the
quantity of soot, that fills the air, is quite
wonderful. Within my memory, our jackdaws
had quite a colour of their own, and their backs
used to shine, like a boot, or a bottle; but now
they go about, as if they swept chimneys.
Emblin, you must have noticed it."

"You have drawn my attention to the fact
before," said his partner, who heard the remark
every week; "but good-bye, I fear, to our
chance of getting off; for here comes a carriage.

Why it is my lord's, and Mr. Gaston in it! What I told you was right; he can do exactly as he pleases, in that quarter."

"I could hardly have believed it," Mr. Latimer replied; "such a self-willed man as my lord was once! But such men seem to become most helpless, when their vigour fails them. It is a lucky thing for him, to have such a man of business, shrewd, active, honest, intelligent, and a thoroughly sound Tory."

"I have not quite the opinion of our friend that you have. However, that is no concern of ours, so long as he has his credentials. Holloa! Why here he is!"

"Gentlemen, your most obedient!" Mr. Gaston exclaimed, in his playful manner, foregoing the honour of being announced. "Delighted to see you, at the receipt of custom. I said to my lord, when he grumbled about something—'You may go all over Lincoln's Inn, Gray's Inn, and both Temples, and find no firm to compare with them.' By old Harry, I was right. And it is not only that, but the manners, the cordiality, the polish put on business."

"Sir, we are much obliged, by your good opinion. What can we do for you, to-day?"

Mr. Latimer disliked familiarity, and was a good judge of a gentleman, inasmuch as he was one himself. But nothing ever abashed George Gaston.

"Well," he said, "I begin to feel ashamed of coming so often, about a thing that seems so simple. But being so entirely trusted with this business, which cannot make the difference of a doit to me, I seem to be compelled to see about it, more than if it were my own concern. Of legal matters I know as little as a babe; and my great desire is to leave the whole of them to you, who know them so thoroughly, and are so careful. But as you know, I am not my own master; and to-day he has been in a perpetual fume. I hope you have settled something."

"I beg you to sit down, sir," Mr. Latimer replied; "you could ill be spared; and there is such a thing as being too hard upon the labouring horse. You have indeed plenty upon your hands, without being worried by this troublesome affair. But let us recount our own little share. Emblin, may I trouble you for the private day-book? Here is a copy of the very careful letter, written by my excellent partner himself, and directed in accordance

with the address which you discovered, by
your most disinterested labours. And here is
that letter itself, bearing all the proper post-
marks, and returned by this very morning's
post, in this new envelope, with a very curt,
not to say discourteous reply. Solitude does
not perhaps improve the manners ; but we
long have known the gentleman to be most
eccentric."

"Short, but not sweet," said Mr. Gaston,
lifting his eyebrows, as he read indignantly—
'I beg to return your rigmarole. Once for all,
I will have nothing to do with the bad lot I
have quitted ; and whether they are alive, or
dead, makes no difference to yours obediently,
L. Arthur.' "Upon my word, such a man is
outside the pale of civilized life altogether."

"So he may be," Mr. Emblin broke in, after
watching Gaston narrowly ; "but that does
not dispense with his signature. The Company
want the land ; they pay a long price for it ;
and it is wholly impossible to convey it, without this gentleman's concurrence, or decease.
My senior agrees with me. The title has been
passed ; and now this fatal hitch arises."

"But we don't want the money, and we hate
to sell the land," cried the visitor, with his red

colour rising. "If they take our land against our will, surely they must take it, as they can get it. Suppose a man could force his land on me, and take my money—should I be bound to show him all the history of my money? Yet how could he tell, that it was my own?".

"In theory, there may be much in that," Mr. Latimer answered gently; "but we must consider things, as they are. These new-fangled companies, they may do good, or they may do harm—which seems more likely; but at any rate they get their Act; and no man's house is his castle against them. They take a man's land, without his leave; and if he cannot make them fee-simple without blemish, they suspend a large percentage of the purchase-money. It is tyranny of course; but if these companies endure, their tyranny will soon be a thousand-fold of that. But to come back to the point,— in the face of this refusal, what are we to do for the best, to meet his lordship's wishes, and to keep things smooth? Is he still under orders to avoid excitement?"

"Sir John Tickell says no more than this, that the banging of a door (unless he banged it himself, which he does pretty heartily, as you know) might send him, in a moment, far beyond the reach of medicine. I wish you would only come, and see him; he still sees old friends, upon his better days; and he has a high regard for you, Mr. Latimer."

"His lordship's remembrance, and good opinion of me," the honest lawyer answered, with a proud glance at his buckles, which had belonged to a Sir Thomas Latimer, "are profoundly gratifying. He is not one who rashly forms good opinions. Even you, Mr. Gaston, were with him some years, before you won his entire confidence. But experience has proved your sterling value."

"I simply do my duty, and deserve no thanks. But it takes a great deal, as you say, to overcome his lordship's mistrust in human nature. A treacherous son is a sad shock to confidence."

"And to lose the better one, a very bitter blow. I see that his lordship keeps his servants still in mourning. It is sad indeed, to see the ancient families die out."

"Come, Mr. Latimer," the visitor said briskly, "there is one old family as young as ever, and one of its finest representatives is here, and I have the honour of looking at him. No compliments, sir; in those I never deal. If I have prospered, and obtained some good repute, and the confidence of every one possessed of noble feeling, it is through nothing more than plain rough truth. I say to everybody, 'you must take me as I am.'"

"But," said Mr. Emblin, who had not got any compliments, and considered his family quite as good as Latimer's, and wanted to be off to see to a little dinner-party, "it appears to me, that we have settled nothing, about the business Mr. Gaston came to speak of; unless it is to leave things *in statu quo.*"

"*Statu quo* is an excellent expression," that gentleman replied, with all his strong cordiality; "it is the proper attitude for large landowners, and their humble representatives. Let the next step proceed from the bold intruders. If they are in a hurry, we are not. We meet them with the simple fact, that we can do no more. They must leap the obstacles, in their own way. Possession is what they want; and they can have it. ' I give thee all, I can no more,' is our final answer to them. You will put the matter in the proper legal form; and there it rests, while his lordship lives."

"But," said Mr. Emblin, who was dry, and very tough, "we are bound to make another effort. This gentleman refuses to have anything to do with us. Perhaps he has a fancy that we have wronged him. None the less, the Company might find him more amenable, especially for a good consideration. Even upon Dartmoor, coin is current. Powderhorn, and Bullrush, are sharp and active people. What do you say to our letting them get at him, as our side cannot do any more, and obtaining his signature, if they can ?"

" An excellent idea," replied Gaston calmly, though his face became purple, and his eyes shone darkly ; " if we could only keep it from his lordship ; and if it were an honourable thing to do so. Otherwise, you know what he would say—' if Powderhorn, and Bullrush, can do my business, and Latimer, and Emblin, cannot, Powderhorn, and Bullrush are the men for me.'"

" Highly as we value our relation towards his lordship, which has now existed for many years," Mr. Latimer interposed, with dignity ; " no fear of the withdrawal of his confidence would hinder us, from doing our duty towards him. That is not the thing to stop us. We never submit to threats. But the step which has been proposed, at a sally, by my valued partner, would not—as he knows even better than I do—be in keeping with professional etiquette. Therefore, sir, we will not adopt the course which you object to."

"How can it make any difference to me?" Mr. Gaston asked, turning round to Mr. Emblin, for he found the calm eyes of the senior partner harder to meet, than the keen gaze of the younger; "I never understand your prim niceties of tweedledum. If I make a mistake, I bow, as every one must do, to such a profession."

"Then let it be so," Mr. Emblin answered lightly, to let the little gust of temper pass; "it is understood, that we do nothing at all, but wait on our oars, till the enemy moves. If he is contented with the title we can give him, all well and good; and let him pay the money. If not, we cannot help it, and he pays into Court a percentage against contingencies. But on no account must his lordship be disturbed, in his present state of health, about it. If anything arises, we do nothing, until we have seen you about it."

"You know better than I do, ten million times over," said Gaston impulsively; "what a plague this business is to me! But when I have once taken up a thing, I seem in some way bound to go on with it. Good-bye, gentlemen, both, good-bye! You are martyrs to business; but even a martyr must not have his dinner burnt, as well as himself."

They followed him to the door, as if they did not quite understand this style of parting. Whether he was going with a friendly turn, or whether he would try—and he seldom tried in vain—to do a mischief to their good firm. For put it as he will, when his stomach is up (and somehow or other, it is most exalted, when profoundly empty) reflection will make the true lawyer less desirous to rule double line, and leave *hiatus*. below the name of a wealthy, elderly, and decidedly combative nobleman. But Gaston spoke no word of weakness, and waved them an airy adieu, upon the landing.

"What do you think he will do?" asked Mr. Emblin, as his partner, without condescending to be seen, observed in a dignified manner the departure of the mighty carriage; "I am sure he is a horribly spiteful fellow."

"I neither know, nor care," Mr. Latimer replied, as he went to get his plodding shoes, and thick gaiters. "He may be very upright; and his conduct seems to prove it. A common time-server would be cap-in-hand to those who are in remainder, and unhappily cannot be set aside. But one thing is certain. He is not a gentleman. He has hurt my feelings needlessly; and it takes a great deal to hurt my feelings. Perhaps, you should scarcely have said what you did. But his observation was simply brutal. Powderhorn, and Bullrush, for his lordship! One thing is certain. We must do nothing, until we are properly requested to do it."

" My little dinner-party will be spoiled," said Mr. Emblin; " and I shall be out of sorts about you too. But clearly you are right. The next move must come from him."

Now it so happened, that this was, to a nicety, the very conclusion desired by George Gaston.

CHAPTER II.

TALL AND SHORT.

THERE was another little dinner spoiled that very day, and by the self-same omnipotent roguery of mankind, exerted perhaps, in the latter case, more frankly and respectably. However, it was sad as almost anything can be, and a far deeper outrage on the feeling of the public, than the rapid demission to their final cause of a hundred hungry lawyers.

To describe this occurrence, without exaggeration, and yet with the sympathy which cannot be refused, is beyond the highest hope of the most sanguine self-esteem ; not only, because no single two persons—if such a phrase may pass in such confusion—to whatever extent they may have both been present (and the whole parish found that it had been present, as the interest waxed, and the danger waned) could upon any terms be brought to reconcile their

accounts with one another's, or even with themselves; but through a deeper denial than that—
for that always happens, and a thing could not
be true, if two people took the same view of it
exactly—namely through a stern, but for our
sakes most beneficial, law of nature, that dogs
have no articulate human speech, as yet.

It was raining cats and dogs—as some loose
genius has discovered to describe it—when
Parson Short, drenched and almost sodden to
the bone, rode up the lane from the village to
his home. The vicarage, a good old-fashioned
house, facing the lowlands, and sheltered from
the moor, stood back in the glebe, at least a
quarter of a mile from any other dwelling, and
from the high-road. Large trees around it kept
out the sun-glare, while they let in the play of
light; and firs of laminated verdure (like the
Deodara that is ousting them) gave a stately
movement to the wind, and divided the driving
rain with shelter.

"My certy, something must be wrong," the
vicar exclaimed, as he found no Thomas at the
gate to meet him (although he was an hour
now behind his time), and what was even more
extraordinary, no *Nous*, with a caper at his
bridle; then he gave a shrill whistle, but neither

man, nor dog, came forth, or made any reply
at all. So he unlatched the gate, with the crook
of his whip, and *Trumpeter* pushed it with his
saturated neck. In a minute Mr. Short was
at his own front-door, but the dripping of the
rain was the only sound to greet him. Getting
down from his horse, with a puddle running
from him, he found the door open; and snatch-
ing a big stick from the umbrella-stand, while
he shouted "House ahoy! Is there nobody
alive here?" on he went to the real head-
quarters of a house—the kitchen. There was
nobody there, and the fire was out, his half-
leg of mutton was floured for the roast, but
reposed upon the table in that interesting
stage; while the dresser, that wholesome pride
of Mrs. Aggett's heart, was in sixes and sevens
of confusion. The master turned pale, for he
expected to find murder, knowing how steady
and how steadfast was his housewife. But in
another moment, great relief ensued, and even
a strong tendency to sad laughter.

For hearing a noise, like that of a small boy
blowing through a papered comb, he grasped
his truncheon firmly, and went to seek it.
And there, in the furthest recess of the scullery,
he beheld a sight such as he never yet had

seen. Lashed to the pump by the long jack-towel, so that she could move neither hand nor foot, was a fat, but highly respectable female, whom he knew by her dress to be his good housekeeper. Her face was invisible, and her tongue under disability, because the metal colander, wherein she was washing spinach, had been securely fastened over, and contained, most fittingly, the whole of her expressive countenance. Upon the upper rim of this vessel, as in a spirit of mockery, played the half-mourning ribbons of her second-best cap, a tribute of respect to the departed Aggett. Hearing her master's approach, she tried to stamp, for her temper was unequal to the strain of this adversity; but the only result was a vibration of the pump, and a little gush of water down her sadly aching back.

With a brief word or two of manly sympathy, the vicar hastened to the knife-box, and finding the game-carver, began to cut the swathings of her long duresse. But when he would have eased her of the dark, oppressive domino, she thrust at him with her liberated elbow, and completing her freedom, made off down the passage. Mr. Short, having lofty opinion of women, looked after her, with a

strong faith in her motives for this rude proceeding. And his confidence was justified, for
no sooner had she found herself round a corner,
where no light shone, than she dashed away the
colander, and screamed back—"No man shan't
zee my vace, till I've washed un." For she was
a fine cook, and she knew how spinach oozes.

"I suppose she knows where Lizzie is; or
she never would bother about her face," the
parson thought, with continued faith; for
Lizzie, the handmaid of the house, was Mrs.
Aggett's only daughter; and before he could
do any more about that, his housekeeper, following the veinage of his thoughts, quicker
than he could follow hers, called back from the
top of the back stairs—"he hath kayed her in.
I've a' heered Lizzie thumping. The black
gentleman have kayed her in your sarmon-
room. Go you, and see to things, it was a
shame on 'e to naglax; and hus'll be down by
that time."

"I fear she is very much put out indeed,"
Mr. Short said to himself, as he went to look
round the house at large; "and what should
I do, if she gave me notice? But this seems
a very queer thing altogether. The plate gone,
of course, and all my money. However, there

was scarcely £50 to steal. Oh, what am I about, to think of miserable money? My *Nous* must be dead, my most clever, faithful darling! He would leap at their throats, till they killed him."

Leaving all his losses to be gained at leisure, he ran out through a side-door to the dog's abode, or rather the stall where he was chained in weather too wet for his kennel; and where he found no comfort but in mourning, when his master was away without him. Mrs. Aggett belonged to that class of women, who from defect of large sympathy, exclaim, " drat the dog! " when they come across a footprint; instead of reflecting on the great superiority of the canine to the human foot, in addition to the double number. And *Nous*, who had no vanity, looked up to Mrs. Aggett; not only because of her control of bones, but also through a sense of her command of broom-handles, such as came down upon him from the wrong direction, and caught him on the back, while he with integrity was gazing forwards. And often he got a great lump by this.

His master understood these woes; and finding consolation grievous, when they made much fuss together, tried to avert the blow by strictest *alibi* of *Nous*, when undefended. For even Mrs. Aggett, thorough despot as she was, durst not descend upon the dog with all her vigour, when the master was at home; and they all knew that. At other times, it was a bitter fact, that if *Nous* came in, with an honest view to luncheon, or a laudable exercise of foresight as to dinner, concerning both the hour and the substance; at the very moment when he stood wiping his feet on the rope-mat, to the utmost of his conscience, a heavy thump of something void of feeling, but capable of conveying it too well, was prone to dim his happiness, and darken his reflections.

"She has brought upon herself this signal Nemesis of pump," Mr. Short muttered grimly, as he ran to look for *Nous*. "There is no rogue in the kingdom, who could steal into our scullery, while that dog was left at large. But why has he not saluted my return? He always hears us coming up the lane. Why, *Nous*, my darling! You are not dead, are you?"

The parson fell back against the stable-door, and a rush of tears dimmed his keen brave eyes. For the poor dog was lying on his side, among the straw, senseless, and motionless, and to all appearance dead. The chain was

jerked tight round his neck, as a hangman's
noose, with the hair standing out from it, and
his body was rolled up like a silkworm spinning,
or a fossil ammonite; while his curly ears, falling back, showed their silver linings, and only
the whites of his eyes could be seen. He had
given up all hope of himself, and only wanted
to die without any more disturbance.

Mr. Short had the presence of mind to say
no more. The dog had not heard him yet;
and to excite him, while he was thus throttled,
would cut his last hair. Stealing his steps,
like a nurse at the bedside of some one afflicted
with heart-disease, the master got behind him,
and looked into the position. After a hard
struggle of long hours, *Nous* was now at his
very last gasp, and he must have been dead
long ago, if he had not managed with extraordinary skill, to get the strongest claw of
each hind foot, under a link of that strangling
chain. To such a strait was he brought, by
simple indignation at the villainy of mankind.

It was impossible to undo the chain, for the
dog had wrought it up into a series of spikes;
but luckily a three-cornered rasp, for the hoofs
of *Trumpeter*, lay handy. Mr. Short took the
twisted chain between his knees, and cut a

link, and eased it at the poor dog's withers, and then released it gently from his puckered throat. Hereupon a little sigh came up, from the huddled hoops of the ribs; and the cut of the nostrils lifted faintly; and the throat began to quiver, with a longing to expel a bark that had stuck fast in it. By great skill and care, he was gradually brought round; but such was his exhaustion, that when he tried to sit up, and lick his master's hand once more, his cramped legs failed him, and he fell among the hay-bands.

As soon as his favourite was out of danger, the vicar (who had shouted in vain for Thomas), returned, in a settled frame of mind, to see how far his household gods were shorn. Being now assured that no life was taken—unless it were that of old Thomas, which appeared scarcely possible to any one who knew him— the master of the premises was ready to consider what had happened, in its proper order. And *Nous*, who displayed much more excitement, because he considered the whole fault his own, came staggering after him, to learn the worst.

Mrs. Aggett, by this time, was evil to approach. She had found her daughter Lizzie, in the sermon-room, crying, not from the effect of the discourses piled around—however touching they might be,—but through inability to escape from them, and the idea of the tombstones which they suggested; in addition to anxiety about her only parent, and a deep inner sense that she had had no dinner. Intolerant of misplaced lamentation, the mother proved the fitness of her survival, by delivering a hearty thump between the mourner's shoulders, then bidding her be off, and thank the Lord, for bread and dripping, she bustled round the house, to see how much was left of anything.

So far as a hasty survey revealed, there was very little gone of any real value. The plate was untouched; but some old-fashioned knives, and notably an ancient Oxford carver (with a heel to it, and a curved hartshorn handle), had vanished; and so had a double-barrelled gun, and a 2 lb. canister of powder, and a stiff three-jointed fly-rod, and a book full of tackle, and a few other things from the lobby of sporting implements. "A must a' been one of they dratted poochers," Mrs. Aggett exclaimed, with great relief; "and welcome a' be to all thic rubbish."

However, when the master came to look,

he found that a little bag of tithes was gone,
containing about £40 in gold, which he seemed
to himself to have hidden right cunningly, in
a hole of his bed-room wall, behind the barometer; which every one was afraid of, as a
piece of wicked witchment. Like a sensible
man, he was vexed to lose his money, although
he had plenty more that could not be stolen;
but remembering at once, that his meaning had
been to spend most of this in charity, he perceived that his charity must be curtailed. But
before he was much consoled by this, he came
upon a dearer loss, which taxed his finest
feelings.

His grandfather, Admiral Short, had been
a person of great punctuality, timing all his
movements by a large gold watch, and thereby
measuring the minutes needful to defeat the
enemy. He was called "Punctuality Short";
because in a contest of some celebrity, he had
said, "we shall have her in twenty-five
minutes;" then holding his watch, with the
going side outwards, upon a nice round abdo-
men, he worked his guns to such effect, that
she struck in 24 minutes 30 seconds. And
when he discharged, with punctuality also, no
more guns, but the peaceful debt of nature,

his last words were, " my grandson Tom is to have the Victory chronometer." A chronometer it was, and beat that of the ship; though portable watches were content, as yet, to be called " watches," and no more.

Finding his money flown, the parson hurried to the case in which he kept this triumph of the Barwise firm. By it, he had the church-clock set; and by it (whatever the church-clock said) he had the bells rung on a Sunday morning, to tell the parish when eight o'clock was; for the women (who always got up first on a Sunday) to put their husbands' clothes out, and for the little girls to soap their brothers, and for the barber—having fifty long beards to hew down, between that and ten o'clock—to pour his boiling water on his dish of suds, and set off to do the halfpenny fellows first. For, as many of the men as paid a penny, got another good hour to stretch their arms.

There were perhaps a thousand things, of almost equal moment, for which this big watch struck the spring—or, if that expression be an involution, awoke the time of day for Christowell. But what is the use of detailing them, when the watch, and all its works, were gone?

It is a remarkable instance of the overpowering effect of great catastrophes, that when Mr. Short found his true Palladium conspicuous by its absence, the only thing he did was, to double his fists unwittingly, and the only thing he said was—" What a bad job ! "

" Hath a' tuk the kay along wi' 'un ? Ay, that a' hath ! " cried Mrs. Aggett, with some admiration, as she came up, to see what her master was about ; " but the zeals be all here. Well, I said a' was a gentleman ; though a' might be a black one."

This observation recalled Mr. Short's attention from the deed, to the doer thereof ; and knowing—as a preacher has opportunity of doing—how soon the clearest impression will fade, he began at once to question his housekeeper, concerning her assailant. And it seemed to him almost to be an excess of her wonted peculiarities, when she charged the blame wholly, and solely, on himself, evincing goodwill, if not downright gratitude, to the man who had fastened her to the pump. The only description she could give, or would, was that he seemed to be " a tall black gentleman, going about very graciously ; " till the vicar at last lost his patience, and exclaimed, " you had better say I robbed my own house. Upon my word, I believe you think so!"

"Noo, noo, twadn't you," the good woman replied; "a' was dree times so tall as you be. 'Twor as much as the odds, atwixt thic, and thiccy." She held up her long middle finger, as she spoke, to indicate the robber gentleman; and then, as figurative of her master, displayed the top-joint of her dumpy thumb. Mr. Short strode away; for if anything annoyed him, it was an allusion to his modesty of stature.

"The poor old woman is so deaf," he pronounced, in a voice quite loud enough to reach her, "that the villain stole behind her, while she was at the sink; and I dare say she never set eyes on him at all. · But Lizzie—Lizzie must know something. And Thomas! Good heavens! is a house to be surprised, and robbed in broad daylight, and the people burked, and gagged, and not a soul be able to tell anything about it? Lizzie, come here, child. You have had time enough to get over your fright, and to satisfy your hunger. Now what was this fellow like, that 'keyed' you in the sermon-room?"

"I can't say, sir, indeed I can't," Lizzie Aggett answered, beginning to whine at the remembrance of her fright; "only he was big, and black, and hugly. If you was to tear me in pieces with wild horses—— "

"Tush!" cried the parson; "was there ever such a set of nincompoops? What became of Thomas, child? Is he in a trance? Was he scared off the premises? Did he see a vision?"

"No, sir, please, sir; leastways not as I knows of. But he seed a half-crown, laying under the laylac, by the stable-door, sir. And he come to ouze, and he saith, 'I must go and see, whether this here be a good coin of the kingdom.' And please, sir, he ain't been back; though I hollered, like a peg bein' killed, out of windy."

"Ah, I understand. I shall have to groom *Trumpeter* myself; if he is to be groomed at all. Run, and see who is thumping at the back-door so."

But the girl trembled so, that the vicar went himself; and there he found the landlord's daughter from the *Three Horse-shoes.*

"Oh, do please to come, sir, as soon as you can," she held up her hands, with urgency; "it isn't raining, anything to speak of now, sir. And your Thomas is that tipsy, in our bar, and laying about him with a pewter pot, that nobody dare go anigh him. We would send for constable, if it wasn't for your reverence. But father saith, to let you know, sir, first; for fear you should take it unkind of us. Father could tackle of him peart enow; if must be. But mother hold him back, by reason of the pewter pot. Your Thomas is a-laying about, so dreadful!"

"I wish he had layed about with equal vigour here," poor Mr. Short muttered, as he set forth again, without a bit of food, and with wet shivers running through him; "bolt the door, Lizzie. Ah, I need not tell you; 'when the horse is stolen,' &c. Don't be afraid, child. They won't come again; for the most rational of all reasons. The Greeks had a proverb, about the great difficulty experienced, even by that most ingenious race, in skinning a skinned dog."

CHAPTER III.

VERY FINE IDEAS.

ACCORDING to many sound opinions—at variance
with others almost as sound—the valley of the
Teign, near Fingle Bridge, is the finest thing
to look at, in the West of England. As in the
vales of Lyn, or Barle, the rugged lines of
Exmoor descend in grace ; so here, the sterner
height, and strength, of Dartmoor fall into
beauty, yet preserve their grandeur. The
windings of the great hills, as they interwend
each other, come down with sweet obeisance
to the shelter of the valley. Their rounded
heights are touched with yellow of scant grass,
or grey of rock ; but under the bleak line, furze
begins, and heather, and oak foliage. With
rapid step, as must be down a pitch of such
precipitance, the foliage slides from tone to tint,
and deepens into darker green. But the play of
lighter colours also, and the glimpse of silver

stems, arise around the craggy openings, and birth of some fern-cradled rill. Far in the depth, short loops of water flash, like a clue to the labyrinth.

All this is very fine, and may be found in many other places also. But the special glory of the Fingle Vale, is the manifold sweep of noble curves, from the north, and from the south, by alternate law, descending; overlapping one another, by the growth of distance, and holding up their haze, like breath that floats, to and fro, between them. These, with winding involution, and recessed embosoming, in fainter and fainter tones retire, to the dim horizon of the heights.

A scene of beauty had many days yet for keeping its rapture to itself; and echoes of solemnity had not learned to exclaim—"come here, Harry," and "oh lawks, Matilda!" Our good British race had not yet been driven, to pant up hill, and perspire down dale, for the sake of saying that they had been there. And people, afoot for their holidays, sought the renown of each place, in the larder.

Of this kind was Sir Joseph Touchwood; a man with no humbug about him, in any pursuit, except that of a contract. "Don't talk to me about your views," he said to his lady, who was picking up all the picturesque expressions; "they don't cost a penny; and they don't bring one in. I have seen some hundreds of them, and was none the wiser. Lazy folk may talk about them. I want my dinner."

"Julia, dear," began Lady Touchwood, who was always more affectionate, in the presence of papa; "do persuade your father, to come with us, for once. It would do him so much good; and he must not always slave." The young lady looked at her father; and perceiving by his lips, that his mind was sternly set, was wise enough not to run the risk of failure.

"He knows best," she answered softly; "and perhaps his mind, instead of relaxing, would only be impatient, all the while. It is happy for us, not to have such a heavy sense of duty; and that he has it. But darling papa will not object to our having a holiday, and asking a few friends."

"You may have all the world and his wife," said Sir Joseph, who was always cross, when hungry; "but no Champagne, mind; only the Saumur; unless Sir Robert Moneywig is quite sure to be there, and to bring his daughter, Chrysolite. After all I have done, and the style you live in, and the table you keep, when I am out of the way, it does seem a little too atrocious, that when I come home, I must keep awake till midnight, to amuse a lot of fellows, who have not got sixpence."

Lady Touchwood, although of fervent spirit, resolved to have it out with him by-and-by, hoping that her daughter would come forward now, and receive a little check to her impertinence. But Julia saw through that manœuvre.

"Do you know why that is, papa?" she asked, with a smile sweetly void of satire. "It is because you are too good-natured, and so extremely amusing. Of course, we all do our best; but still, none of us can talk as you do."

"You have not been through such things as I have," replied Sir Joseph, who could talk of nothing, except the weather, and the price of corn, and leather; "if you had, with your abilities, my dear, you could describe almost anything. Oh, dinner is up, is it? And high time too. If Master Richard appears, just tell him, he may go to the pantry; he shall not come in to us. There shall be punctuality in my house. When I was a boy—oh dear, oh dear!"

"Hush!" said Lady Touchwood—or at least

she "breathed it," according to the fashion of expression now. Too often, Sir Joseph would flout the stately air of his "princely apartments," with sudden reminiscence of the days when he was hungry, and the things he enjoyed, with his apron on. His daughter always laughed, and said, "do tell us more;" but his wife, as a matter of duty, quenched it.

"Now I do not wish you to misunderstand me," this strong-minded baronet took care to say; when the dinner was over, and he began to spy about (in a full frame of mind) for his pipe, and round chair, and the clearance of the women; "what I said was plain enough. If you are certain, that Sir Robert means to be with you, take half a dozen of the very dry champagne, and for the girls the sweeter stuff. No Saumur; I would not have it said; and the name is on the corks, confound them! I heard of it once; when I myself took the labels off the bottles. An idiot said—but I will not spoil my pipe. Under any circumstances, take champagne. Julia will count, how much there is. But open no 'Extra Sec,' until you see Sir Robert, and his daughter, with those wretched old screws they keep. Mind, I wish things to be done handsomely, and in accordance with my reputation; if anybody comes at all, who is capable of judging."

"All shall be done, to the very utmost of my poor ability," his daughter replied, as she rose to fetch his pipe, and the ancient brass tobacco-box, which had cost him a penny, when pence were scarce. Then she drew towards the fire his favourite chair; for a fire was still a comfort, and however grand the room might be, where he dined, there he would have his pipe, and in no other chair but that. Cushions, and sloping backs, he hated, but loved this old ashen seat, which was not even polished, but closely railed round the back, and cupped in the centre, and supported by six substantial legs.

Whatever might be said against Sir Joseph, his bitterest enemy, or the man who got the worst of him, could scarcely describe him as a "stuck-up cad;" for his common sense kept him from that disgrace. His "social duties"—as his wife and daughter called them—were the greatest pest of his life. He felt that he had earned, as well as needed, his nap on a Saturday eve, and his curtained pew on Sunday, and the bliss of not having to listen, while people talked of things, that concerned him not. Yet, with the vigour, which had led him to success, and the patience which confirmed it, he was ready to go into his best clothes often, and show the hospitality, for which the West was famous.

But his strong sense of duty failed to carry him into this "Gipseying;" as outdoor parties away from home were called, in that more simple time. The money, and provisions, he would furnish; when convinced that other wealthy people had to do the like, and when allowed to grumble without any contradiction. Outside his own desk, it was his chief ambition to settle his daughter Julia well, for he was really proud, as well as truly fond of Julia. And to hear that she had enjoyed herself, and made a good figure among rich people, and to receive a grateful kiss from her brightly smiling lips, was very nearly as good to him, as a sounder investment of the cash. Therefore, when he got his pipe that evening, he said that they might go as far as five and twenty guineas; so long as they bothered him no more about it.

Miss Touchwood at once resolved, in private, to stick at nothing short of fifty guineas, if she could manage to spend so much; for she wished to make a stir in the neighbourhood, and arouse a spirit of lively competition. And she managed

to persuade her dear papa, that this noble
scheme would at once release him, from giving
grand dinners, for a month to come, and also
relieve him from the great-gunned assault,
setting in upon the most sacred arches of his
cellar. For a canon of Exeter had discovered
(Providentially, as he told his wife, who said—
yes, that was the proper word; for his dear constitution required a fillip) that, in the cellar at
Touchwood Park, lingered still a ruby shadow
of the finest vintage ever known, upon the Alto
Douro,—the finest, but the scantiest, when the
grapes were trodden by the war-horse. It was
a wine distinctly placed far above the range of
lay understanding; and the canon (though
strongly adjured by Mrs. Botrys, to confine his
discovery to his own bosom) in a genial discussion of some bottles of his own, with a brother
canon, and a prebendary, frankly referred to
that loftier standard; and a meeting of the
Chapter was held, next day.

"You may still save some of that dry old
stuff, from the even dryer people who come after
it," with such words Julia consoled her father;
" by giving these gipseyings, instead of dinner-
parties. Even a canon cannot expect port, so
early in the day, even if it bore the carriage;

and they don't know anything about champagne. Papa, you might get a lot at an auction, or smuggled, at about a pound a dozen. Nobody would suspect you, and nothing could be fairer. The Government try to cheat you always; and you have a right to cheat the Government."

" Julia," said Sir Joseph, with a deep interior twinkle, which might have been interpreted— 'instruct your grandfather in the suction of gallinaceous products;' "my daughter, it is better not to say such things, even without meaning them. Persons, not conversant with my career, and slow-mouthed at making, or taking a joke, would misunderstand you, and stare, and talk about it; whereas, if there is one rule of the very highest principle, it is to have no words about a contract, made for the nation's good, and carried out with energy. I have a bin of very ancient Hock, possibly a little beyond its prime. The sourer it is, the more the clever people smack their lips. Work it off first, my dear; you know some words of German; nobody else does, and it will prove your schooling. Half a pinch of snuff; and then the chair to put my legs up."

The lady of the house was not best pleased with her daughter, for coming forward so.

"What do you know about such things?" she asked. "If you take any more upon yourself, you may take all. I shall stay at home; and you may put all the invitations in your own name. No doubt that would be the proper thing to do, according to the style the chits of girls are now introducing, from America. Don't say another word. I won't go."

This was rather awkward; but the clever girl got over it, and smoothed down her mother, to sweet interest in the matter. And the most delicious invitations, such as ladies alone can write, convinced everybody who received one, that the whole success of a daring enterprise hung upon his, or her, acceptance. And more than that, everybody wanted to be there.

"Oh I do wish that I could go," cried Rose, running with a letter into "Naboth's Vineyard," as she wickedly called the last hobby of the captain, because she had not the free run of it; "it is such a glorious idea, father dear! And to think of my getting such a sweet invitation! All of it is done to please you, of course. But I know how hard you are, to please."

"And how easy to displease," her father answered smiling, with his thoughtful face rather red from stooping; "an Ogre, a Draco, a child-devouring Saturn. Show me this honeyed invitation, Rosie, that my malice may find an outlet. By the Poles, how affectionate the lady is! 'Darling Rose!' Whose darling are you?"

"Papa, I am so glad, whenever you are jealous. But read on. Do be fair for once."

"'Darling Rose,'" read Mr. Arthur, with well-feigned wrath, well softened off; "'for *really* your kindness to my *dear son* compels me to cast off formality—will you do us yet *another favour?* In the quietest of all quiet ways, and with one or two *delightful people* coming, chiefly dignitaries of the Church, we are going to that *most romantic* spot, Fingle Bridge, next Thursday. We propose to do nothing more than *look about*, with an interval of mild refreshment. It has been said that we should refresh our taste for the *grand and the beautiful*, more often than we do. I scarcely understand what such things mean; but *I feel*, when they tell me, that I am *bound* to do it. If *Captain Arthur* could be induced, by any sense of duty, to join us, how he would *enhance* our pleasure, and be able to explain, to the reverend gentlemen, the names of the trees, etc.! But that, I fear, is a *hopeless thing.* Only do coax him, for I am quite sure that you *can coax* irresistibly, to let *you* come to this *most secluded* party; and a carriage with a lady-friend of yours inside it, Miss Perperaps, the daughter of the doctor, will be ready for you, at your *private gate,* at *ten o'clock, on Thursday.* Ever gratefully, and truly yours, Mariana Touchwood.'" Her church-name was 'Mary Anne.'

"Now it is a pretty letter, and full of generosity," Rose exclaimed, with the fervour of bright youth; "and so kind of them, too, to invite Sporetta. I like Sporetta, she is so straightforward; and if she had been at a good school, she would have been the cleverest girl you can conceive. Oh, how I do wish, I could go!"

"Stop! Here is a postscript about your friend. 'We have not asked Spotty yet, and do not mean to do so, unless we hear that you will join us. Julia Touchwood.' What do you say to that, my child?"

"Well, I think that whoever put that in must be candid, and truthful, but not very nice. Miss Touchwood is a very great beauty, I believe; but I don't think I should like her.

As regards Master Dicky, they owe poor Spotty, at least a hundred times as much, as they owe me. And they should have invited her, first of all. I don't care at all, about going now, among such ungrateful people."

"You are a most hot-headed little creature," Mr. Arthur answered, though his smile undid his censure; "but look at it in another way, my dear. Possibly Miss Perperaps longs to go most awfully (according to the phrase they all use now, but which I especially object to), and if you decline, you destroy her chance."

"But, papa, I was sure that you would never let me go."

"Oh then, that was why the grapes were sour! My darling, I cannot bear to rob you of every enjoyment, for the short time such enjoyment lasts. You have never seen the loveliest spot round Dartmoor; and I think that you ought to go, for your friend's sake. Neither of you has much change of scene, or chance of harmless pleasure. I particularly wish you to go, my Rosie."

Filial duty was her strongest point, and she could not bear to ask for money. Her father also, being light of cash, and a man of rather lofty temperament, took a large and distant

view of the things belonging to the outward
female, and too often absorbing the inward
one. Now and again, he would give her a
bit of something to match with her sweet
pretty self, and he praised the results of her
own handiwork; but a good round sum, to go
to Exeter, and sit down with, on one of those
wondrous high shop-stools, was not beyond his
compass only, but wholly in the vacant distance
of imagination. The subject demands even
less to be touched with extremest reservation,
than to be run away from, by people who have
not studied it. And the safest thing is to quote
feminine verdict, in a question for female jury.

"Lor a' mussy," Mrs. Pugsley cried, when
the young lady went through a process of
careening, after the accident at Moreton; "Tim,
her hathn't got a hook and eye, about her!"

Husbands, in a great degree, fathers, in a
greater one, are well content with their own
contentment; the which is a saving virtue.
"Gew-gaws utterly spoil your appearance,"
they declare right nobly; "take my word for
it, my darling, that nothing could improve
you." But the darling likes to take other
words as well, and is reasonable in doing so;
while they all despise extravagance.

"Father has stumped up a five pound note. I knew where it was, and I gave him no peace," said Spotty to Rose, while there yet was time to make up things, if you could only get them. "What do you think, I said to him, dear, when he took the key out of his box, with a bang? And I knew very well, who put him up to it. She is in such a way about not being asked, that I only get cheese-rinds for supper, ever since. I said, 'Very well; it is no concern of mine. I don't care twopence how I look. I shall go with Dicky Touchwood's bandages on. They came from the valends of the broken down bedstead. And there is quite a beautiful fringe to them. Starched up, and plaited, they will look quite grand. And perhaps Master Dicky will not recognize them. If he does, he will know they are in the bill.' I wish you could have seen my dear parent's face. But I am very glad you did not hear what he said. How much is the captain going to stump up?"

"My father has a very large mind," said Rose, who could not help laughing, though sadly shocked; "I never dream of speaking to him, in such a manner."

"They have all got large minds, to save their pockets," answered the impious Sporetta; "but you can't go, in anything you have got. Tell the captain, you will go with your night-gown on."

"Miss Perperaps, if you talk so coarsely, I shall decline to go with you."

"Very well. Go in sack-cloth and ashes. I will sit on the box, and leave you all the inside. That stuck-up Julia will be delighted, to see you look such a perfect fright. She knows you are ten times prettier than she is. And she is after some young fellow, who dotes on you. Oh my! Wouldn't I try to cut her out, if the Lord had made me handsome?"

Miss Arthur did her utmost to repel such low ideas; and she would not even deign to ask, about any gentleman, called "a young fellow." Without any arrogance, and purely from her own distinct ideas of right, and wrong —which come down, in questions of behaviour, to be called good manners, and bad manners— she had found that Spotty Perperaps did not suit her. And no low taunts, about being a frump, or a dowdy, had any effect upon her mind, whenever she brought it up strictly to the question.

"Come down, Rosie, here is a box for you," her father shouted up the stairs one day, when she was doing Arachnoid work, in the quarters of a Sunday frock that suffer most from piety; " tenpence to pay, and you to pay it; and Master Pugsley vows that he can't afford to book it. Hunt up your purse, and come down, and pay; if you will do things so recklessly."

" I have not got tenpence in the world," cried Rose; " how very unkind it is of people! It must be the old books, I left behind; and I am sure they are not worth tenpence. But I have got fourpence, if you can only manage to lend me sixpence, till next time."

" What a fine expression !" Mr. Arthur answered, looking up the stairs impatiently; for he enjoyed, like a child, the assault of pleasure; " when will next time be ? Come down, and have it out with the carrier."

" Niver you be in a hoory, Missy," Pugsley advised, in his leisurely way. " I be allays in a hoory, and my life gooth out o' me, by rason of dooty; but you be young. It's Pugsley here, and Pugsley there, till there bain't a button of me left, to answer. Lor, if I wor to go and cut a cord like that—wutt be you about, Miss Rosie ?

There have been gunpooder, at the tail of Teddy."

" That makes him go so fast, I suppose," said Rosie, who was getting much excited by this time; " my scissors won't go through this cord. I am not going to pay tenpence for nothing; and you may take it back, and try to get twenty pence, at the other end. That is the law of it, about the letters."

" Her dothn't know nort about the law; no more nor I do. Please to pay up the tenpence, Missy. I be vast to-day, I be." The carrier favoured the captain with a wink.

"The only way you can be fast," she answered, " is when you stick fast ; as you did the other day. What makes you in such a dreadful hurry now ? You shall have the ten-pence, if the things are worth it."

" Many's the time it hath been my lot," Master Pugsley went on heavily, " to carr' tuppence-worth, and have to ax tew shillin'—presents and sichlike, from rich folk to poor ones. But carryer must have 's money, all the zame, whether a' bringeth good vally, or no. Please goo, and vetch the tenpence, Missy. Teddy can't baide no longer."

" I never knew you show such a mean,

greedy, avaricious spirit. Oh, I beg your pardon, heartily, and humbly! I had no idea that you could play a part so well."

Master Pugsley exploded, as none can explode, but a Devonshire man, who has corked himself down, and corded his cork on a joke of his own brewing, mellow, well-seasoned, and full of body. " Wull'e strike, agin' paying the tenpence now?" he asked, with the tears of laughter reddening on his cheeks, from the purple ground they ran upon; though a fine sense of humour would have scarcely bred a smile, out of that common material, surprise. But Rose, instead of joining in his laugh, was hard put, not to burst into tears ; such a power of shame arose, through her delight; because she had been cross at pure kindness.

" I am very sorry—it was all your fault. I never saw anything so lovely, in my life. Oh, father, you must have spent a hundred pounds ! I don't deserve a thread of it. Do let them take it back. It is only fit for some great Princess."

" It is fit for you, my child ; and you for it. Or at any rate, I hope, the things will fit you. I had not the least idea, in my stupid way, that you were so badly off for clothes. But good

Mrs. Pugsley has enlightened me; and your kind school-mistress managed all the rest. So now run away. Let Moggy take the box up; and by-and-by, come and show me, how you look."

CHAPTER IV.

GIPSEYING DAY.

It is too hard upon a quiet little village (where
everybody knows, twice a day, how everybody
else's cough is; and scarcely can the most
industrious woman find anything to say, that
she has not said thrice) suddenly to be swept
off its legs, by a hurricane, a water-spout, an
earthquake, and a thunderbolt, all coming down
upon it, in one clap. To say, that Christowell
suffered all these things at once, would be
scarcely true perhaps, at any rate for the present; although they were soon to come bodily.
But even now a heavy strain was put on the
constitution of society; and folk who had
scarcely had a thing to talk of, going on now
for a twelvemonth (except the Post-office, and
its insolence), were now flung into this deeper
pit—that they did not know, what to talk of

first. Who can deny, that this is by far the more dangerous of the two extremes ?

There are, in history, periods when the popular verdict is of value; but these are of very rare occurrence, and are not to be forced, by most dexterous use of the powerful implement of Samson. Good men may be knocked down, by that, and bad ones hoisted into their seats, and the rogues prevail, by the prevalence of fools. But, upon the heels of pale ignominy, ruddy dignity returns at last; and the nation pays cheerfully an enormous price, for recovering the power of blushing. Because it feels itself, to be again a nation.

Not far otherwise, at Christowell, faction (headed by the cobbler, tailed by the tailor, and stomached by the tripeman) had wriggled up a wretched little insurrection, against faith, honour, and dignity. But no sooner had the people seen what such things led to, by the insolent robbery of the vicarage, and the cording and colandering of a female (whose tongue was universally respected), than a wholesome, and hearty revulsion ensued. Trickey, (who had long ago been waxing over-haughty and vamping himself up, with office, and stamping on the young Queen's head, destroying of her picture,) had aided, and abetted the felony, to the utmost of his power, by delivering the letter, which alone had prevented the parson from shooting the perpetrator. The tripeman, in spite of all the rain, had been out with his dog-cart; and that looked bad. And though the tailor had stayed at home, he knew best what his reason was. As soon as the planks across the water, (which the flood had washed away), were replaced, unanimous opinion met upon them; and the men sat down, to let the women use their voices. And by such means, everything became so clear, and the merits of the vicar so victorious, that if any of the three anti-clerics had been up to " Malicious height "— which has since come down — the constable in the next parish but one, who went to Petty Sessions, would have heard of it.

Even as no man can be looked at, without having knowledge of it—though it be but the spinal seam of his coat, that receives the impact —so these three men, before any of the others had smoked a pipe, perceived the feeling in the air about them. They met together, and then came out, laying aside all sense of rank, and even of money owing to them, in their strong indignant manhood; which grew more indignant, as conscious debtors grew more deter-

mined not to see them. Suppressing success-
fully all sentiments of cash, they addressed the
public, which already was ashamed; for the three
men had their best coats on; and what they
said, was to the purpose, and without a wasted
word.

"Dothn't Mother Aggett zay, 'twor a gentleman, as dooed it?"

"Her doth; her doth. Her be zure of that,"
the public, from all its planks, replied.

"And hath Mother Aggett had oppurtoonity,
to jidge of a gentleman, when her zees 'un?"

"Ay, that her hath. Her hath a' been in
vaine vam'lies, let alone Passon Shart's."

"Well then, doth ere a wan of us dree zim
laikely to be taken for a gentleman? Spak the
Lord's truth, and no lies now."

"Never a wan of 'e; by a blaind man, nor a
deaf 'un; lave alone a 'ooman, as hath lived in
vam'lies."

Without another syllable, of reasoning or
reproof, the cobbler, the tailor, and the tripeman turned, and marched all abreast to the
Three Horse-shoes; and shame alone stopped
their calumniators, from hastening after them,
to drink their health.

But this episode, instead of allaying, served

only to enlarge the ferment; and the scores of
rumours, that took wing daily, proved—if such a
thing requires proving—that the slow mind is
the most inventive. All, however, was invention; without a stroke of discovery; even though
there were as yet no police, round Dartmoor, to
handcuff discovery. And Mr. Short, in his brief
way, said that detection is like dining; if a
man wants it done, he must do it for himself.

In this fine spirit, he resolved to go, though
most people said that he ought to stop at home,
to the party of distinguished gipseys, about to
encamp at Fingle Bridge. " A vast amount of
chaff must be met somehow," he thought, with
a knowledge of that material, partly derived
from his dealings therein; "and I had better
meet it in the lump. They will shoot their
brilliant flight so thick, as to knock one another
out of aim. I shall fail to understand them;
till they explain their jokes. And a joke ex-
pounded, is a joke confounded. And it will be
a treat, worth a lot of heavy banter, to see Rose,
and Julia, meet."

Discharging his duty still, as parson of the
parish, he had been to see Miss Arthur's new
apparel; a foretaste of which had astonished him
in church. And superficial though his learning

was, in matters of that high nature, or art, he
had contrived to give, as well as to find, a refreshment of soft pleasure. For the maiden's
innocent delight (not only in comely, and taste-
ful attire, but also in her own fitness for it, and
above all, in her father's loving kindness) was
enough to please any but a very churlish
person, and to tempt forth many a smile of
praise. Captain Larks looked on, with resigna-
tion; having heard the same things said, fifty
times now, and making his mind up to complain
of tautology, when he had heard them a hundred
times.

"Suppose, it should be a most lovely morning,
as lovely as even this *liliet* of something," said
Mr. Short, while Rose turned round, to escape a
tea-leaf on the carpet; "and then when everybody is up on the hill, where there is not a
furze-bush for umbrella—one of our Dartmoor
storms comes on."

"Oh, Mr. Short, you have sent such a shiver
—I mean, you have startled me so sadly. And
you are always right, about the weather. Please
to say, that you do not mean it."

"Far be it from me to foretell such woes : I
never pretend to know anything, about the
character of the day after to-morrow. Even to-

morrow has beaten me now; for I never expected that day of deluge, when my little house was robbed. But somebody else did, and made a fine thing of his weather-lore. Whoever it was, he foresaw a great rain; for the letter was posted the day before, and he knew that my house would have no one near it; he sent me away, and the place was at his mercy. He knew more of the weather, than I do."

"That alone ought to supply some clue," Mr. Arthur broke in upon their lighter talk; "or at any rate, it restricts your search. It must be some fellow, almost living on the moor, and out of doors perpetually, who can beat you and me, in the weather signs. I know them pretty well; you know them better; but the weather beat both of us that day. I would have bet ten to one, especially after the way I saw the trout rise, that the day would be fine; but now I remember,—yes, I saw some worms expecting; and a frog had got his hind-legs crossed."

"When the tadpoles go up and down——" said Rose. "But who are we, or who are they, to beat all men of the loftiest science, with centuries of instruments to help them? It seems too bad, that——"

"You had better wait, my darling," Mr. Arthur said, for fear of her turn of mind becoming scientific—the uttermost disaster that can befal a female; and Rose was already beginning to know a barometer, from a thermometer, and the north-east wind, from the south-west; "my Rose, you had better wait a little, and consult the tadpoles, instead of Mr. Short."

"The tadpoles know a great deal more than I do," the vicar acknowledged, with the candour of a man, who has been mistaken lately; "but they turn to croakers; and I will not. Let us hope for weather, as lovely as all the pretty things, that will be there."

When the day came, there were many pretty things "come to see, and to be seen"—according to one of those grand "examples," which abide in the mind, when the rule is lost, in the dissolution of Syntax. But though a round dozen —and round they were—of Devonshire beauties came to the scratch (to adopt Mr. Short's low metaphor), all, except every single one of them in private, confessed that they were only fit to hold a candle, to Julia Touchwood, and Rose Arthur. Upon such a question, a good bold statement is better than elaborate description.

And, as to the palm betwixt those twain, Julia was sure that she ought to have it, but wanted to get her opinion confirmed; while Rose, without dreaming of any competition, admired Miss Touchwood's dress, very, very candidly.

When they met, in a beautiful path of the wood, with the officious Dicky fetching them, there really was a nice piece of manners, as well as a pretty interview. Either had heard of the other so much, and formed such imaginary portraits, that both were a little excited; but one thought it wise to conceal that condition; while the other never thought about it.

Julia Touchwood had long intended to be "garbed with simplicity," at this feast of nature; or as our best authorities express it, to be "dressed with studious plainness." But her mother, with the eagle-eye of the superior sex, had found a hole in this, or made one. "You want to look, as if you were not come out. You may try that, after thirty; but at your age, you should try to look older."

"I shall suit myself," the young lady replied; and truly she had done it. She was just in that interval of the ages—if such an interval there be—when the velvety half of the human race take superior views of apparel. Therefore, it was not to please herself, but others, that she had a new costume from Paris imported by her father, and so refulgent, that the custom-house people winked every eye.

"How charming it is to discover you, at last!" Miss Touchwood exclaimed to the sweet simple Rose, as if she had lit upon a flower in a hedge-row. "You have been so wonderfully kind to my dear brother! Dicky, be off. We want to talk." Dicky made a face, and desired to stop. But the weight was against him, and he had to go.

"But I have always been at home," said Rose, as quiet, and truthful, as her pearl-grey dress, which was of some material unknown to Julia, soft, and supple, and of mild sub-lustre, yet void of shrinking, and fast not to run; "I have always been at home, Miss Touchwood; except on the day, when you happened to call upon us. And you understood, that I could not call on you."

"I did not expect you; and that makes it all the kinder, on your part, to be with us to-day. I hope to introduce you to some very famous people. Their names might frighten you; but when you come to talk to them, they scarcely seem to know anything at all; or if they do, they keep it very close. I always expect to be amused. Don't you?"

"I have never thought about it, in that kind of way. It is so seldom that I go from home. And at home I have so many things to do. If you will kindly allow me, I shall be much happier, without being introduced. There are several people whom I know here; quite enough to keep me from feeling lonely. And this place is so lovely, that it seems a shame to talk."

"Why that was the principal thing we came for," Miss Touchwood answered, with a lively smile; "but you shall do just as you like; unless the bishop comes, as he half promised to do, if his many engagements allowed it. If he does, you must be presented to him; because it is lucky for young people."

"Oh, I know the bishop very well indeed; he has always been most kind to me. If he comes, I shall go at once, and see him."

Julia, with all her good manners, could not help looking, and almost expressing, her surprise; while Rose coloured deeply, not because of the bishop, but through fear that she might have spoken rashly.

"She has told a great fib," was Miss Touchwood's inference, sped by her sense of a small one of her own; for she knew that the bishop could not come, and fancied that Rose might know it too. However, she only said, "Oh, you know him? How delightful he is, when he likes to be! And he does love trout. Have you heard of my clever brother Richard's scheme? A diversion, in the best sense of the word. Mr. Short is in such a fume about it! Has Dicky told you? He is in such glory!"

"He is full of ideas," said Rose most gravely; at which the other laughed most merrily. "Yes, he is indeed; when he could not shake his foot, he spent most of his time in inventing."

"No wonder he talks about you so much, because of your noble faith in him. He has invented one thing, I believe, the only thing he ever will invent; and that is perpetual motion. What a plague he must have been to you! He wears me out of my wits sometimes, even when he ought to be as tired as a pack-horse. But his present invention is not his own, or at least it seems much too good for him. It certainly is a very fine idea; for it helps on the day, at so many turns. He wanted to bring fifty terriers here, and treat all the canons to a rat-hunt; but of course we would not hear of that. So he struck out this new light, which promises much excitement. People call him stupid; but I do not. If he were stupid, could he get at least fifty rough men to admire him, and to obey his orders?"

"He has an extraordinary gift of being liked," said Rose, with a smile, for she liked him herself; "especially with the labouring men. Our man, Samuel Slowbury, very rarely indeed is wide awake. But your brother formed a friendship—I beg your pardon, an acquaintance with him; and Sam can scarcely sleep, if 'Squire Dicky's' name is mentioned."

"Just so; that is the state of feeling in our house, and round it. And he has taken advantage of it, to order his army in this direction. At the hoisting of a flag where the two paths meet, at least five-and-twenty men are to descend from Cranbrook Castle, where they keep their beer, with shovels, and two-bills, and all that, on their shoulders. And nobody is to know what they are to do, until they have done it, and the result is ours. I hope I have roused your curiosity. But if you meet Mr. Short, try not to ask him; for he thinks it a hundred-fold worse than the lashing of his Mrs. Aggett to the stake—I mean the pump.

I must run away now; but I shall look for you again; and don't forget your promise about the bishop. I shall send some one, to keep you in view. You have got your sketch-book; I shall claim one."

Rose, being left to herself, or at least with none but strangers sauntering near, turned up a steep, and zigzag path, which seemed likely to lead to a fine view up the valley. Here she was obliged to be very careful, as her pretty dress was in frequent peril; but without mishap, she gained a corner, where a glorious opening shone. At the just height, and the proper turn, to catch the long avenue of winding vale, a grassy knoll gave standing-place, and the obstruction of the wood sank down into copse, that only paved the foreground. With a short breath of wonder, and a long one of delight, Rose stopped, and sat down by a low whortle-bush, with a pink frill still adorning it. Before her were folded, and unfolded, the long hazy windings of the Fingle vale, the loveliest view that had ever filled her eyes. The perfection of beauty made her sad; she threw down her useless drawing-book, and hung upon the turn of thought for tears.

Suddenly vigorous steps came near, firm

steps that sounded not unknown; and before she had time to look bright, and thoughtless, a young man was gazing at her, with profound surprise. Good manners told him haply not to notice her confusion; but love, and love's sympathy, got the better of good manners, or in nature bettered them. Without formality, he took her hand, as if she wanted caring for.

"Why are you sitting like this, all alone? And with tears in your eyes! Have any of those stupid people dared to be rude to you? Or has that poor little Hop o' my Thumb——"

"No, he has been very good," she answered, forgetting that she should have asked, who was meant. "I am as happy as possible here. Every one has been most kind to me. I did not expect to see you, Mr. Westcombe."

"And I scarcely hoped that you would be here. I knew that you had been invited, but —well, I came in the forlorn hope of it. Is your good father here? I fear not; because you are never far apart."

"No, there was no chance of his coming. If he went out once, he would have to go always, because everybody likes him so. Lady Touchwood would have been more delighted than she could describe, as she very kindly told me; but it was useless to think of such a thing. Now wasn't it kind of him, to let me come?"

"That it was; especially to me. You know, your father is always most kind to me. And he told me, that he liked me."

"Are you sure that he did that? It does not sound like his way at all. I never knew him say that to anybody." Rose looked up doubtfully; but Jack was sure about it.

"You must not tell him that I boasted of it, because he would think me so conceited; and perhaps it would set his mind against me; which I do hope you would never try to do. I never yet saw any one I liked so much—I mean of course counting up the gentlemen I know, and leaving out the ladies—as your dear father, my dear Miss Arthur. And he certainly felt some good-will towards me; though not to be spoken of,—I mean, not to compare with my intense admiration, and affection for him."

"But you have only seen him once!" said Rose, looking, as if her father ought to produce these grand impressions at a glance, but did not always do so; "how can you have managed to understand him so entirely?"

"Because the gift runs in our family," he

answered, with the vigour which comes of believing a thing. "My father has got it twice as much as I have, because he has seen so much more of the world. He is down the hill now. He finds his legs a little stiff. He has been a good deal shot about, and bayonetted in three places. But he wants to come up, if there is anything to see; and he sent me on first, to make sure of it. Please to stay here, just where you are; and look like yourself, when he comes up; I will have him here, before you have time to think about him. It takes a long time to think about him."

"How fond he does seem to be of his father! And how much he admires mine!" thought Rose; "it is a very rare thing, they say, to meet with such high principles now."

Not only did this young man now take stand on a very high level of principle, but he carried out with vigour filial duty, and helped his father up the hill. Almost before Miss Arthur could get into a nice indifferent state, and absorb her mind upon the landscape, John Westcombe came into view again, with one end of a long stick in both hands, and his dear father's hat at the other end rising. "Stiff work, stiff work; don't pull too hard. It is worse than any Spanish mountain," the elder gentleman panted forth; "don't be in such a 'hurry, my dear Jack. We have got all the day before us."

"Allow me to introduce," said Jack, excited beyond all filial bounds, "my dear father, Colonel Westcombe. Miss Arthur, this is Colonel Westcombe!"

"Lugged in at the utmost disadvantage," said the colonel, labouring to make a flourish. "But, bless my heart, I know you, my dear! Shake hands, while I think how I came to know you."

"I am certain," said Rose, with her bright blushing smile, as he took both her hands, and admired her, "that if I had ever met you before, sir, I should not have forgotten you."

"And yet I have forgotten you? Well put! That would be a disgrace to me. No; I suppose it was but a fancy. My memory begins to play me tricks. But if I do not know your face, I know its expression; and it does me good. It does me good to look at you, my dear, and to think of the days when I was young. There are very few lovely faces now. The young ladies are so pert, and forward; and that spoils the prettiest face in the world.

Have you been drawing? And may we see it?"

"No; I could not even tell where to begin. I can only draw a barn, or a linhay, or a stile; great distance, and grandeur, are beyond me altogether. I know what I can do; and what I can't."

"Then," replied the colonel, who rejoiced in common sense, "you know the most important thing, there is for us to know. It is just what the young ladies never seem to know now; nor even the old gentlemen. I am very much afraid my son will tell you, that I don't, for one. As for him, he does not know what he can do; and he is too bashful to find out."

"I like to hear my father talk," said Jack; who had been observing, with intense delight, the conquest of the colonel, by the maiden of his love; "he positively hates conceit, and no one can have less of it than he has. Yet one of the foremost objects of his life, seems to be —to make me conceited!"

"We must not trouble you, at first sight," his father said to Rose very gravely, meaning thereby to rebuke his son, for intruding family politics, though himself had set the example; "with such little discussions, as we have at home. When we have the honour of knowing you better, there will be time enough for that. But why are you sitting here all alone? Has any jealousy on Julia's part—I mean have they contrived, for some young ladies are not entirely above all tricks, to put you aside, to shelf you—as we say, with any one no longer wanted?"

"Quite the contrary. I ran away. I am so accustomed to be alone. A crowd of strangers bewilders me. I have scarcely begun to enjoy this view yet. Have you ever seen anything more beautiful?"

"Never; at least of its own special kind. But we are interfering with your enjoyment. It was not my fault, it was my son's; though I must not blame him, for so pleasant a surprise. But promise me one thing, if you are not engaged, allow me to take care of you, when we meet by-and-by. I don't know what the arrangements are. But after the great engineering scheme, the fires will be lighted, and some cookery ensue. I mean, if the rain should have the manners to keep off. My old friend, Short, says that it will pour before six o'clock; and he is nearly always right. We must hope for the best. What would all the ladies do?"

Rose promised gladly to place herself in such good care; and upon that pledge, they left her, and returned to the gay folk in the valley.

"Now you understand why I brought you up," John Westcombe said, as they were going down the hill. "That is the young lady, I mean to marry; that is to say, if I can. If I don't, I shall marry nobody."

"I never heard you speak like that before, and I think you might have asked my leave, or (if that is out of date) my opinion at least," his father replied, rather sharply for him. "You remind me of our great commander. She is a very sweet, and charming girl. But I must know a great deal more about her. How did you make her acquaintance, my boy?"

Jack told him all about it, and all that he could tell, without breaking his pledge to Mr. Arthur; and the colonel's brave eyes shone with softness, when he heard of what Rose had done. "A noble girl! A most noble girl! I am not surprised at your infatuation, Jack," he exclaimed as he shook his son's hand again; "but you must not be in such a hurry. Such maidens are not to be won in a moment. Moreover, I must know more about her, or at any rate about her father. Keep out of sight, for the rest of the day; and leave her to me entirely. I shall manage better than you would."

This arrangement was not at all to the liking of the younger gentleman; but he could not oppose it with any good grace, when his father had just been so kind to him. But before he had time to think much about that, or make any promise about it, a great patch of yellow was seen betwixt the branches, waving and flapping, over Fingle Bridge. "It must be a flag of 'keep away,' as we used to call it," said the old soldier to his son; "perhaps there are gipseys there, and small-pox."

"No, it is a flag of 'come on;' a signal for the men on the hill, and for us to assemble. The 'great piece of sport,' as Dicky Touchwood calls it, or, as Mr. Short describes it, 'the atrocious bit of poaching,' is now to come off, for our enjoyment. That flag is the handkerchief of Canon Botrys, a bandana as large as a table-cloth. He is famous for them, and for his knowedge of port wine."

Colonel Westcombe felt a deep interest in this, for he always liked to follow up such questions, and had often heard of Canon Botrys.

"He deserves, then, to fly his own flag," said he.

But no time remained for discussion of the canon's merits, or of even more important subjects; for spectacle, and action, at short notice, took the place of dialogue.

"You are not to go, until they have begun. I beg of you, ladies, to be good enough to keep back; you will be in the way, and get frightfully splashed," Dicky Touchwood was shouting, again and again; but the ladies were determined to be in good time, and were zealously hurrying one another. For Dicky had been too proud of his scheme, to keep his own counsel about it.

"If you will only wait a quarter of an hour," he cried in despair, as the ladies still rushed on, "I will have a path cut for you, such a nice path, that you will be able to get along, without the least danger to your dresses. But now—oh, dear, there will be such a lot of mending!"

At this, the ladies only laughed, and bore on all the faster; and a saucy girl called back to ask, if he thought she had never been in a wood till now.

"There won't be a fish, not a single minnow

even, if you go ten steps further. Upon my word and honour, it is too bad, after all my trouble, to be laughed at!" So hot was his wrath, that he strove to get in front of the ladies, to bar the way; but the track was so narrow, and the ground so steep, that without a rude push he could not do it. And Dicky was more polite than they, as a host, and a gentleman must be. But suddenly, the ladies met their match.

A shortish old man, with hedger's gloves on, and a rip-hook swinging in one hand, confronted the fair troop at a sharp corner, where the narrow path overhung the river. " Yew baide there, till nex' taime," said the old man, planting a sheep-hurdle, stuffed with furze and briar, under the saucy young lady's nose, and proceeding to lash it, with tough oak frithles, to a pair of stout ash-saplings; "so zoon as Maister Dicky hath had one of 'e a bit, a' wull know better than to razon wi' a vemmel." Having fastened his hurdle at the foot as well, John Sage proceeded with some more important work; and the ladies confessed themselves beaten, for the moment.

" The wood is full of vipers newly hatched," they said to one another, with their usual knowledge; "and even if one could get out of their way, there is no getting through the vile brambles." So they made up their minds, that there was nothing worth seeing. Nevertheless they were all very angry, or, at any rate, pretended so to be; until they were called to their first refreshment, which proved most satisfactory.

"Now come and see my engineering," cried Dicky, running down the path, in a reek of mud and water, as one who had been labouring, the while they were indulging; "no pop-stuff for me, no thank you! One glass of ale, and I am off again. Mr. Short, you call yourself a great fisherman; come, and see me catch more in one hour, than you will catch in the whole course of your life."

It was villainously true; wicked advantage had been taken of a doubt of the river about its course, where a violent flood had once endeavoured to cut short a gentle winding of the glen. "It ought to be straight," Squire Touchwood said, with a true Briton's love of brevity; "between its extreme points, it has no right to go twisting in that clumsy way. I will get the man's leave, and do it for him. We will invite him to see it done. It will improve his property ever so much; and if he behaves well, he shall have some fish." So Farmer Crang came down, to see what they were going to do with him; and he lived upon so steep a hill, that when he had to go home at night, it kept on knocking him on the chin, much as he tried to keep above it, while feeling that he meant what he had a right to do—to get to his house, at the top of it.

But that happened later. At present, he belonged to the Rechabites, for at least twenty minutes, in spite of all the ladies coming up to him with glasses. But when he saw a cork go up, like the rising of a lark, into the sky, Farmer Crang said, "A' must be zumthin undernathe 'un. I winder if a' wud make me go up." It made him go up, for a brief elevation, and come down sadly afterwards.

Therefore, the whole thing was a great success. Without taking anything to raise their colour, the ladies were refreshed into a finer peace of mind; and the gentlemen took heart, and tried to please them. And in excellent spirits, they all set off, to see the great spectacle, now prepared. For the river, running under Fingle Bridge, was ruddy with more than legendary slaughter, or muddy perhaps with the stir of many "navvies." Miss Arthur, inheriting some little share of her father's love of solitude, and as yet unaccustomed to wine and noise, had been wandering in the wood, while the luncheon went on, with a quiet young lady, whose acquaintance she had made; and even Jack Westcombe had failed to find her. But now, she came down, to see what was going on, for fear of being thought rude and odd. At once Miss Perperaps, who had been doing particularly well among the bottles, ran up and embraced, and scolded and fed her, and turned away the other young lady, and led her to behold the engineering feat.

Alas the poor Teign, like the Achelöus, or the river that offended Cyrus, had been turned out of its ancient bed, for nearly a quarter of a mile. At the head of a long loop, a dam had been piled, while a channel was cut into the heel; the dastardly water, perpetually labouring to degrade itself most rapidly, rushed down the new cut, and deserted the old, with all the bosom-friends enshrined in it. These, in their honest faith, never could believe that the sweet haunts of childhood would bewray them; and they said to one another, as the banks went up, and their own swimming places seemed to go down very low, that here must be a new form of drought, beginning with dreadfully muddy water. But the elderly trout were not satisfied with this; they knew that the world is full of angles, and they hurried up and down, to learn the meaning of it all. Unluckily for them, they added nothing to their wisdom; if they went down stream, John Sage stopped them, with all his descendants wading gladly; if they darted up stream, things were worse, for thick legs in worsted stockings were puddling all the water. Therefore they assembled in their pools, to think about it. And this was as stupid a thing, as they could do.

Men are so prone to think about themselves only, and from a higher view endowed so largely with contempt of what other beings think of them, that scarcely more than two minds, of all the many present, dwelt with any feeling on this outrage to the fish. Mr. Short was shocked, and so was John Westcombe, from that love of fair play, which is bred of manly sport; and these two would not even go to see what happened, neither would they taste a fish thus murdered. Rose Arthur also thought it a cruel piece of business; but Spotty was in ecstasy, and dragged her on to look at it.

To describe such a villainous slaughter of

trout, would be almost as bad as to share in it. Enough, and more than enough to say, that these poaching scamps got as much as they could carry, with two strong donkeys to help them; and the only piece of luck was that Canon Botrys, in his greed for stewed eel, got his thumb bitten through by a patriarch of that nimble race; and his circulation being somewhat thick, congestion ensued, and he was put upon gruel, without even a spoonful of crusted port to flavour it, until the following October. Sir Joseph Touchwood heard of it, and was truly thankful.

But for the others there was vengeance also. Every one of them became a fish, or wished to be one, for several hours of his life that night. The rain avenged the river, not by sheer wrath only, but also by a subtlety of fine skill, and high finish. Astutely it began, as if meaning nothing beyond a drop or two to lay the dust, and to set the birds singing, and the young men winging their umbrellas for the maidens of their love. The leaves, now growing to a steadfast colour—for oak-apple day was come and gone—took only as many drops as they could hold; so that eyes under new bonnets might be lifted up, and admire them, without fear of wet response. "How lovely they do look in their tears!" exclaimed a young lady in sky-blue silk.

"But I hope they won't cry too much," said Spotty.

Laying aside further dread of that, when Prebendary Woolfleece (who kept a rain-gauge) staked his reputation on a lovely evening, all the company, full of bright alacrity, assembled, in the open space below the bridge, to fry their great hoist of fish, and cook their other dainties. Lady Touchwood (who had kept as much out of the way, as was possible for the feast-lady, by force of many good reasons of her own) came forward now, to show her daughter's fearful ignorance of the soundest of all accomplishments. The fires of furze made a beautiful blaze, succeeded by a sweet glow of embers; frying-pans abounded, and bladders of lard, and jars of very lightly salted butter, and any one, with the rudest rudiments of knowledge, was at liberty to try his hand, or hers, or both together. They did it; they did not care what came of it, because they had nothing to pay for it; and supposing a trout to be coal on one side, and as raw as a candle on the other, they found out some part of him done very nicely, and praised one another's cookery. And more engagements, with a view to matrimony, were made, before it began to rain again, than had ever been heard of in so short a time, or than parents approved, or than ever came to anything.

In this witching hour of the time, with gentle feelings, and genial smells beginning to pervade the valley, and the sparkle of the sun upon the lightly sprinkled leaves contributing myriad playfulness, Jack Westcombe, who never had been capable of coping with the growth of the age in facetiousness—the cuckoo, that has ousted both wit, and humour—was looking as if he would like to take one of his hosts by the neck, and lay him in a frying-pan. The desire was natural, but far from just; for Dicky was behaving in his very best style, and for the good of the company. While laid up so sadly, and yet so sweetly, at Lark's Cot, he had found out that Rose was a ministering angel at the frying-pan, and especially in the last offices of trout. In right of this knowledge, he brought her forward to a central pan upon the embers, where the poor creatures were being murdered again, by an elegant lady from Exeter. But Rose, though her heart was aroused at such a sight, drew back, with the sensitive recoil of genius, until the other lady upset the frying-pan, and ran away to make a boast of it!

Then Miss Arthur was moved beyond her wont, and resolved to do things properly; for the substance and spirit of good work were in her, and slur and waste were an outrage to her mind. Without a word of anything, she tucked her sleeves up, so as not to leave a crease upon them, and she asked for some butter with no salt in it, and a cold frying-pan without seam on the bottom. Bad work cannot be turned into good; any more than wrong can be turned into right, in this world. Men of great learning came up to help her; but she only bowed, and begged them not to do so. Only, for the sake of her frock, she accepted Archdeacon Barley-corn's offer of his " long front "—who came to an apron afterwards—to save her *liliet* from rockets of the fire capricious. Then she busked up the fire; for it is not good to have too slow an ember, neither to let the pan sit down on it; and then—it would be very unfair to say how —she fried trout, so that they were grateful. And (as every one who does good work, in this age of slur, gets over-worked immediately,) from every other bonfire, fish came pouring; and the Chapter came to an appetite again, by

sniffing, and beholding laymen eat; and Dicky
Touchwood was in ecstasies, and Julia loftily
sarcastic. For Sir Robert Moneywig had just
arrived, and his daughter Chrysolite shone most
grandly.

Colonel Westcombe watched all these things
duly, in his quiet well-contented style; while
Mr. Short bustled about among the ladies,
allotting to every one her proper period, as if
he still carried his grandfather's watch. After
these duties, he foregathered with his friend,
bringing a bottle of the " Extra Sec," intended
for the great Sir Robert. " Now what do
you think of those three girls," he asked,
" Miss Moneywig, Miss Touchwood, and Miss
Arthur ? "

The colonel, in a personal question like this,
made a point of forming no hasty opinions;
unless he was downright forced to do so, by
indignation, admiration, or some other power
that stormed his judgment. In his active days,
he had waited to be told what he was to do;
and then he always did it.

" Short, you know as well as I do. They
are all very beautiful girls," he said. " How
is good *Nous?* Is his throat-wound gone ? "

" Now don't attempt to put me off, like that.

I have told you all about him, long ago. Much credit to you, that such things should happen. They have made you a Justice of the Peace; and you must stir. But I will know your opinion of my lovely little Rose."

"She is no little Rose, she is a fine tall girl, and very soon will be a beautiful woman. I will not say a word against the others. But even while she works, see how she walks! No Devonshire maid can walk like that. When I was a young man once in Spain—but never mind; all has been ordered for the best."

"I should hope so. You villain, how dare you sigh? But here comes something, both to sigh for, and to groan; as old Farmer Pook said in church, when I exhorted my hearers to sigh for their transgressions. 'Dunno the way to zaigh,' he shouted out, for I happened to look at him, as I spoke; 'our vam'ly always groanies.' And here comes a groaning time for all young ladies. I told you all along, what it would be."

CHAPTER V.

EGYPTIAN NIGHT.

Now all these people—and there must have been a hundred, of the polished material, and as many of the rough, according to the division now in vogue—had thoroughly enjoyed a very pleasant day, and could scarcely expect, as reasonable beings, to enjoy the night as well. Without slaying a black sheep, in honour of the wind, or a white one, to propitiate the moon, or even paying heed to weather-glass, they had ventured, at a risky time of year, into the stronghold of bad weather; and they did not even bless their stars, for the luck so far vouchsafed to them. So they wanted a lesson, and they got it most impressively.

Having made an exemplary mistake of late, and paid for it with his chronometer, Parson Short (although boldly prophetic to the colonel) had refused to do more than shake his head, when the ladies consulted him about their clothes. The wisest of men loses faith in his wisdom, when it has cost him a lump of his tithes, and suspects a vein of irony; as the Pythia might have done, after failing to predict her own robbery. But now there was no possibility of mistake, to any one acquainted with the manner of the moor. "Have you brought your close carriage, as I told you?" asked the parson.

Colonel Westcombe replied that, much as he disliked to be shut up in a box on wheels, he had come in his wife's carriage, both to please her, and to help any women who might be in trouble of the rain.

"There are lots of great people here," said the parson, smiling wickedly, "without so much as Tim Pugsley's poke, to protect their sumptuous raiment. Not one of them will bear the idea of being soaked, although they all have courted it. The Touchwoods have two closed carriages here; but the hired things (such as Rose, and Spotty came in) are as open as a net; a tarred net is their similitude. With half an hour's rain, they drip black drops, that never come out, though you wash and wring, for ever. Little Rose deserves a better fate than that. How lovely she looks in her silver grey! She has not the least sense of the rain impending; and rain, and ruin, are the same word to her frock. She will cry; for she never had such a frock before; and she won't care twopence for its value perhaps, but for the disaster to her father's kindness. Your carriage will be besieged by mighty ladies; but they can afford to get tarred every day. Make Rose go with you, and put her in first, and dare her to come out, and put your terrier on her cloak; or else they will turn her out, or sit upon her lap; those ladies are such tremendous crushers."

"Short, I have known you for twenty years," said his old friend, looking with surprise at him; "but you are full of unknown corners still. See to it all yourself. I cannot perceive any ground for rushing into action, before completing my dinner. One reason why we generally got off pretty well, was that we seldom went into action with empty bellies; as our brave foes very often had to do. What we had was tough; but we got through it, and were fit for tough work afterwards. Ah, there will never be such days again. Our muscles stood up, like stubs of wire, and our teeth would go through heart of oak. How well I remember an old Spanish cock, when I had the honour of dining—but perhaps, I have mentioned that to you before."

"Scarcely less than fifty times. The tale has an improving tendency; and I wish there were time for another edition. This lamb is excellent, and eke the lobster. Take a bone with you, like an old campaigner; and get your horses in, as soon as may be. In a few minutes, there will be helter-skelter. Here comes the swirl of air, that outruns the storm. I will bring Rosie to the road across the bridge."

"Now, don't you get in front of Jack," called out the colonel, as the parson made off, with the wind behind him; "Jack must learn to do the proper business for the ladies. You have had your time, and let it go by. Leave Rose to Jack; she is too young for you. You may do the best you can, with Julia. Don't hurry me. I won't be hurried. What are these petty drizzles, after the mountain-storms I have had to encounter, for whole weeks together? True it is, that I was younger then——" he added, as his hat flew away into the river; "but never mind, I can always tie my head up. The rising generation is a wonder; but if they lose their hats, their heads go too. Equally hollow both of them."

Colonel Westcombe very seldom said a spiteful word; but it was enough to vex him, to see his new beaver display no swimming power, in the rapids of the Teign; and to hear a loud laugh from some young fellows (meant for gentlemen) who, if they had been at all up to their birth, would have jumped into the water, and pushed one another out of it, in rivalry to help a white-haired man. The colonel, in reply to their laugh, bowed gravely, to thank them for having observed his trouble; and then, with deliberation, walked into the river, found his water-logged hat, and without another glance at them, crossed the rugged channel, to save going round by the bridge, for his horses. Jack Westcombe, who was watching Rose, saw by her glance that something was wrong in that direction; and as soon as he found out what it was, indignation made him act amiss. For he took the two leaders, in the heyday of their grin, and re-called their jocularity to their own concerns, by delivering them handsomely into a lively stickle.

Scarcely was there time to get fairly through this, before the full brunt of the storm was upon them, and the valley was swept with confusion. The hills seemed to bow in the darkening air; and torrent wisps, like pitchforked hay, covered all the lines of wood, and crag. Away went canvas, kettle-poles, and hampers; and not even a bottle full of stout could keep its heels. The ladies, who would not heed a word of warning, clung to the trees, and strove to bring their skirts behind them; for skirts were then worn, where they now have heel-flaps. Like arrows a cloth-yard long, thickened in with cross-bow bolts, came the flight of the rain, with a cast of blue among the tree-trunks, where it ran into the forest haze. Where it struck the young leaves, they went up, like shells, with the glazed side downward; and any brown folio of last year, still sticking to its musty chronicle, was whirled and tossed off, like a winnowing.

But one of the worst things, for all the good people, who had fed on the fat of the land all day, and plucked every flower of the valley, was the rising of their ashes, into their own eyes, and teeth. Stacks of dried furze from the hill had been burnt, to enable them to spoil

cookery, and many a poor tree had been harried
of its young leaves, by their skeltering smoke.
And now, being full of intelligence, they owned
—whenever they found space for a whisper—
that there is such a thing as paying dearly for
one's roast.

Young Westcombe had observed, with much
vexation, that through Squire Dicky's manœuvre
about Rose, his own good father had been
robbed of the pleasure of her company, at dinner-
time. After all the kindness of Mr. Arthur,
and the confidence placed in his honour, Jack
had felt, throughout the day, that it would be
mean on his part, to take advantage of this
neutral ground, and endeavour so to steal into
forbidden graces. Nevertheless, it had seemed
quite fair to bring about, as far as might be, a
feeling of good will, and independent liking,
between the fair stranger, and the colonel. And
now, when he saw the hope of this cut short, in
the general confusion, and nobody coming to
the aid of poor Miss Arthur, his heart burned
within him, to redress the sad neglect. Without
a moment lost, he ran up, and led her into a
beautifully sheltered spot, where a cove of dry
stone was overhung with fringe of ivy. "You
never think twice about yourself," he said;

" they have roasted you, and run away, and left you to get sodden."

" It is not quite so bad as that," she answered, while the storm increased around; " I am not even wet; and if I were, it would not hurt me, except for my father's kindness."

" How fond you are of your dear father! I am sure, I am not at all surprised at it. I have met him several times; and I feel as if—but he does not want any praise of mine."

" He is far above anybody's praise," said Rose, lifting her gentle eyes with pride; and then for fear of seeming rude, she added,—" but I am very glad that you speak so; because you are so straightforward."

" And what did you think of my father, if you please? You have not seen him at his best to-day. People of this kind put him out; because he is so unpretentious. I was in such a rage, when they called you away, just when my father would have got on well. It was too bad of that little miserable Dicky. I would gladly have put him on the bonfire. I hope he is drenched by this time."

" You should not say such little things. I am sure you do not mean them. He is not well yet; and he is never very strong. There was such a rush of dust, that I cannot be sure; but I think I saw Lady Touchwood, in the distance, putting him into the great yellow carriage, with a tall man to take care of him. He requires to be well looked after."

Jack Westcombe laughed, for he was greatly pleased. Young men seem to have no confidence at all, either in their own choice, or in the judgment of the chosen one; or why do they continually get so jealous of some fellow utterly below contempt? "You scarcely seem to share his dear mamma's opinion of him," Jack became quite noble, as he cast off petty feelings; "but, Miss Arthur, there are many things about him, that one cannot help feeling an affection for. He does not give himself half the airs, that might be expected of him. He is very kind-hearted, and he loves his bit of sport, and he tries to set up a strong way of his own; if his mother, and sister, would only let him. He won't take to cheating, like his father,—at least, that is not what I ought to say; what I mean is, that he does not love commerce, and contracts, and those dishonest ways of getting half-a-dozen carriages. He is soft; but by way of contrast, I like him. Squire Dicky is not a bad fellow at all."

Rose Arthur looked at Jack, as he shook his head judicially, after summing up in favour of Dicky Touchwood; and she wondered at his impartiality about a gentleman, whom he had longed so lately to put upon one of the bonfires. Somehow or other, she had formed great faith in the stability of this Jack; and now he seemed a Jack of both sides.

"You must not suppose that he will ever do anything," continued the other, for fear of having helped to exalt his rival dangerously; "he will never do any good, as long as he exists. Only it is a great thing to do no harm; for people who have gone up so, and made a heap of money. But you have not told me, what you thought of my good father."

"I never saw anybody I liked so much, without knowing anything about them. He seems to me to be of the very noblest nature; and he had just come up a tremendous hill!"

"He can go up a hill now, every bit as well as I can," said Jack with filial poetic licence; "if it wasn't for his wounds, I could never overtake him. But that is a trifle, compared to what they say about him, in all the great histories. In at least three battles with the entire French army, everything depended upon my father ; and he did it so superbly, that their only chance was, to run away immediately. He never mentions it ; and he would be very angry, to think that I knew anything about it. But history is history, and there you find the whole of it. Though I should not have known half as much as I do, if it had not been for old General Punk. The general is a most opinionated man, and a great friend of my father's ; and when anything is said, he shuts one eye, and just glances with the other at my father. If you could only see him, you would understand how our old officers conceal their exploits."

" I have always thought, and I am quite sure now," cried Rose, blushing up to her long eyelashes, as she dropped them in sweet excitement, " that my father must have done great exploits too ; because he never speaks of them. He was in the thickest of the war in Spain ; as I know from a quantity of little things, about olives, and grapes, and cork-trees. But oh, Mr. Westcombe, I never meant to speak of it ; and I beg you not to say a word about it. My father's desire is to live in strict retirement ; as nearly all the great men long to do. I may trust you, I am sure, not to say a word about it."

" Your father has trusted me," Jack answered,

with a gaze magnanimously calm, and abstract,
considering the state his heart was in ; " I know
a great deal more of him, than anybody else
does. He said, that he could see what I was
quite plainly ; and I do not violate any confidence, in telling you that he liked me."

It may be doubted, whether this was purely
upright, on the part of Mr. John Westcombe.
And he even felt some doubts upon the point
himself, when he came to think of it afterwards.
But for Rose to be looking at him, as she was,
and for him to be looking at her, and knowing
how seldom he got any chance of so doing—
purely through his own uprightness—and feeling what a difference it made to him, even to be
near her, in the very worst of weather ; and
what a thing it would be, to have made her
think a little of him, just now and then, with a
gentle bit of sympathy, and a soft curiosity
about his thoughts—all this, in one moment,
crowding in upon him so, left him very little
time for neglecting his own interests.

" If the rain would only stop," said the young
lady, looking round, for something superior to
talk of ; " but it seems to be growing darker,
almost every minute. It serves me quite right,
for my selfishness in coming."

"You should never say that. You did not
come, to please yourself; but because your
father wished it. Leave everything to me. I
will take good care, that you shall get home
quite dry, and very nice—though nothing could
make you look anything but nice. Now will
you be frightened, if I run away, for less than
ten minutes; and will you promise strictly to
stay here?"

She laughed at the idea of being frightened;
and nodded, with a pretty smile, her promise
to stay there. "But I am so afraid that you
will get wet!" she said, with a glance worth a
thousand thorough duckings. In fear of making
answer too impulsive, Jack kissed his hand, and
set forth into the storm, wishing hotly that
there was a hurricane, or deluge, to meet for her
sake, and to shield her from. And she came to
the corner of the shelter, and peeped round,
with her beautiful hair scattered down the outward shoulder, and her hat blown back, and the
carmine of the wind striking the oval of her
gentle face.

"Go back," he shouted; and she obeyed him,
and thought of him, the whole time that she was
left alone.

The age of our country was already falling

into that querulous dotage of finicking, now so universal in the toothless time; but still a young Englishman was ashamed, to put himself under an umbrella; though ·now his only shame is, to have one too large to be taken for more than his essential parasol. Jack never knew—for love was still existing—whether it rained, or blew, or thundered, or whether an earthquake was running in the neighbourhood. The only occupation of his mind was, to consider the doings of Rose, and the sayings of Rose, the lookings of Rose, and the thinkings of the same, whenever they were not past finding out. And he never said to himself—"I may be a fool;" the wisdom, or the folly, of himself was never mooted. His heart was gone entirely beyond his mind's discussion; and the two agreed to let it be; so long as they were happy.

"Why, Jack, my boy, you look as if you had just come across an angel," Mr. Short exclaimed, in his unromantic style, as Westcombe rushed in, among a score of people fighting for a dry place, until they got their carriages; "come along a little way, and I will introduce you to Canon Botrys, and our good Archdeacon. Young men should never miss an opportunity. I know a man who got a living, because his handkerchief was dry. You ought to be in orders, and you shall be yet; because it is too late for anything else. They are under a wall; and they have got nice daughters. You will go away, without having seen a single soul."

"I have seen everybody in the place worth seeing; and I don't know how to see souls;" Jack answered, with a rudeness unusual to him; but the levity of Bachelor Short was distasteful to his feelings. "All I want to know is— where is our trap, and where is the governor?"

"Let me put you up to a little thing, Jack," the vicar replied, with a turn of kind thought, which the young man had scarcely earned of him; "if you want to keep a seat, in your good father's carriage, for some one very nicely dressed, and likely to shed tears at the drops of tar-water, let the other flys, and rumbelows, come down first. The ladies will rush into the first that come; without two thoughts of owner-ship. And the colonel is so polite, that he would let them pack your carriage, up to the glasses, and order him all about with it. You would never get home to-night, to begin with; and you could not squeeze even Spotty Per-peraps in, not to speak of any other well-dressed young lady. You twig me. Ha, see the first proof of it!" A lumbering fly came down; and was crammed, four on each seat, before the horse could stick his heels in.

"Thank you!" cried Jack. "What a clear head you have got! Mr. Short, I beg your pardon. You have obliged me greatly. But keep Miss Perperaps for our carriage."

In another instant, he was running up the hill, just in time to stop his father's carriage from coming down it; though the colonel, defiant of all rain, was on the box. "Draw aside a bit, I want to speak to you," cried Jack; and his father obeyed him, for he saw that it was earnest.

"Take the reins, and manage it yourself," replied the colonel, as soon as he had heard what his son's idea was; "I dare say you are right; and it would please me more, to save a poor young lady, than a dozen of these grand madams, who have fifty fine dresses at home."

"She never thinks twice about her dress," said Jack; "she would look just as well in a potato-sack. It is only because her father was so kind about it. Miss Perperaps told me the story; and I hope to have her with us also;

because she is not very rich. Father, jump inside, you are very wet already."

By this good management, it was brought about, that the colonel, and Miss Perperaps, had the carriage to themselves, and Mr. Short stood by the horses, while Jack, with a great pile of wrappings, went to look for his beloved. She had obeyed his injunction to stay there, and added such a pretty blush of pleasure, to her look of gratitude for his thoughtfulness, that he scarcely knew how to protect her enough.

" Please to remember one thing," he said, as her dimpled chin protruded from his mother's carriage-fur, and he took the liberty of asking for a pin ; " unless you keep quite close to my arm, through the wood, everything will blow away, and my father will abuse me. He always says, that I am so clumsy, whenever ladies are concerned."

"Then I doubt, whether he can understand the subject ; or, at any rate, not so well as you do. You have done everything, to perfection ; and I shall never be able to thank you enough."

In a quarter of an hour, Jack was driving up the winding hill, towards Drewsteignton ; a very long roundabout road, but the only one fit for a carriage towards the moor; while Mr. Short fetched his own horse, and faced the storm, up the steepy track, that climbs to Cranbrook Castle. "I shall be at Christowell, long before you are," he had called in at the window, as he saw Rose sitting, in a happy condition, at the colonel's side, and Spotty set up opposite, in a grin of lively comfort. "Young ladies, shall I tell your dear parents all about you?"

"You had better not," cried Miss Perperaps audaciously; "we are all right now; and we want them to get anxious. My pa would be very anxious, if he dared."

"I shall tell your dear step-mamma, that you have been drowned; it will be such a shock to her—when you come home alive."

Spotty was delighted with this tantalising prospect; and she had such a real style of laughing, when she did laugh—which was not very often, for a frequent is a feeble laugh— that the parson, in spite of all the weather, caught it up, and said to himself, as he rode away briskly, "I know a good many young fellows, who might do worse than marry Spotty Perperaps. In the dark she looks almost as well as Miss Arthur; and we mortals spend most of our time in the dark. I must get up this hill, though, before it grows darker; or down I go through the tree-tops."

For the gloom of night was closing in; so that the valley seemed to deepen, and grow narrower, with the folds of the storm-cloud sweeping through the hollows, the clevices of crag thrown forth, by the bowing of trees to the wind, and the patches of gorse-land darkened by the soaking rain. Jack West-combe was fain to urge his horses up the hill, that he might get past the dangerous places, before the last of the daylight waned.

"What a shame to let him get so wet!" said Spotty, who very soon dropped formality. "You must have brought a coachman, Colonel Westcombe, or a footman, or somebody."

"Only one man, to look after the horses; and I lent him to some ladies, whose driver had enjoyed the refreshments of the day too heartily. I fear there will be many accidents to-night. Six casks of XXX, from Dunsford brewery, was an error of judgment upon Master Dicky's part. However, have no fear about my son. He gets wet upon the moor, con-tinually."

"What an extraordinary thing," replied Spotty, who liked to give the world all the benefit of her shrewdness, "that your son should know the road, on this side of the moor, so well! I thought that you lived, all away by Okehampton. There is no carriage-road, in that direction, from our village."

"Well, now you speak of it, I am surprised a little. Jack is always riding, or walking about, here, there, and everywhere, without much object. His dear mother calls him a Jack-of-the-lantern. But that would not teach him these roads, as you say; but rather the places where there are no roads. However, he seems to know his way right well. He has a most wonderful memory, that young man. It would be wrong for me to praise him; but I never meet any one, who does not admire his abilities, and what is far more, his discretion, and steadiness, high principles, and truly noble feelings."

"He seems to know how to drive, at any rate. Don't you think so, Rosie, dear?"

"I know so little of carriages, that I cannot pretend to be a judge," answered Rose. "The only carriage I understand, is Mr. Pugsley's tilt-cart; but I have a very slight acquaintance also, with Mr. Short's yellow four-wheeled gig."

Colonel Westcombe laughed, and took her hand in his. "I like you very much," he said, "because you are so truthful. Your father must allow you to come, and spend some time with us. I have heard, that you have no mother; only a good father, to whom you are greatly attached, and who lives a very quiet life, just as we do."

Then suddenly Rose (who had never found time, in the hurry and flurry, to think about it) discovered, that this most kind and loveable gentleman, looking so gently at her, was Mr. Short's friend, whom he had wished to bring over to see them, two or three months ago. She ought to have known it long ago; but her mind had been occupied so entirely, with the many new impressions of this strange day, that the one perception, of most importance to her own little world, had escaped her. Now if, through her selfish stupidity, her father's indulgence, and confidence, should recoil upon him, in the very result which he feared the most, better had she never beheld this day. Better, at any rate, would it be, to walk the many miles of rain and darkness, than to bring to her father's door the man, whom least of all he wanted there. She longed to jump out of the carriage at once; but a second thought showed her the folly of arousing curiosity, by an outrageous act. So she leaned back in the darkness, with a miserable mind.

"You do not answer me, my dear," said Colonel Westcombe, in his quiet winning tone, as if he sought a favour; "perhaps you are thinking, that I should have asked your father's kind consent, before I spoke. If so, I believe that you are quite right. I spoke, on the spur of the moment, from a wish not only to please myself, but to add to the happiness of my dear wife. Her health is not at all what we could wish. She is quite unable to meet rough people, or even our general visitors. But she loves a gentle face like yours, and a soft voice, and sweet quiet ways. And I am sure, you will not think me rude in saying, that no young lady would be the loser, by the friendship of one so good, and kind, and motherly, and wonderfully well-informed."

"Oh, I know what it would be; I have very often felt it. It is the very thing that I should like most dearly," Rose answered, with a little sigh; which vexed her when she thought of it. "But there are always troubles—or at least, I should say obstacles—I cannot express myself

very well, I know—but I thank you with all
my heart; and you will understand me."

"It is the way her pa shuts her up," Miss
Perperaps explained, reaching forward to the
colonel, as if he were deaf, as well as stupid;
"the very same thing, that my step-ma does
to me. Only I do want dragooning, I admit;
because I am awfully fond of pleasure. But
she—you might put her in a bucket, and wind
her up and down a well, all day; and she
would smile, every time she came out at the
top."

"You are a remarkable young lady too," said
the colonel, looking, with new interest, at as
much as he could make out of this quick movement, which came to his shirt-frills, and then
jerked back; "you seem to lose no time, in
making up your mind, and if possible, less in
declaring it."

"That's my card. I am sat upon a good
bit; because my pa must go, and have another
sort of wife; when I was doing bloomingly.
But I am beginning to come round; and now,
they find me hot to sit upon."

Of all the things Colonel Westcombe loathed,
slang from a young girl's lips was foremost.
The girls of the present day fancy it a new

thing, and a " rise " upon their elders, to patter this vile English. If they knew, that their grandmothers were beaten out of all that stale stuff, in their infancy, perhaps they would eschew the nauseous trick.

" Are you an intimate friend of Miss Arthur?" Colonel Westcombe asked, without showing surprise; "and did her father entrust her to your charge?"

" I am not half so thick with her, as I should like to be. I scraped acquaintance first, professionally; and I haven't got much further now; though I like her. And as for her coming under my wing, colonel, there is not a year between us, I believe; and we both came under the Reverend Short; but he was spoons all day, on Julia."

The elderly man was made quite happy by this explanation; for he knew the deep obstinacy of his son; and how love even screws down the lids of blind eyes. And it would have made a sad want of echo in his heart, if his only boy had loved a girl capable of being " very thick " with Spotty Perperaps. Then, his generous nature told him, that he had wronged Miss Arthur, by the questions he had put; and he scarcely saw how to let her know it, except by endeavouring to find her hand again.

Her hand was trembling, when he found it; for a tallow-candle, stuck in a blacking-jar, and twinkling through lozenges of green glass, revealed the toll-gate on the Exeter road, within a mile of Christowell; and the poor girl could think of no device, for keeping this carriage from her father's gate. Very soon, a splashing, and a grinding sound announced the crossing of the Christow ford, below the village; and then Spotty called out, "There's my pa's house! Highly genteel, with a red bull's eye. Hold hard, mister; and thank you very much."

Miss Perperaps, after shaking hands with the colonel, bounced out, and rang the paternal bell; while Rose made a quick attempt to follow, but without a rude push could not get by. "No, no, my dear; we will take you to your own door; or as near to it as we can get," Colonel Westcombe said decisively; "this is not a night for walking, one step more than can be helped. Drive on, my boy, as far as Mr. Arthur's. Don't tell me about the road," he continued, as Rose began imploring him not to risk his carriage; "if Pugsley can go there, so can we. Gee up, coachey!" Jack (though he had his own misgivings as to what might come of it) aroused his nags with a cheerful flick, which made them sidle into one another; as men do, when the whip is in the air; both for the sake of sweet sympathy, and that the other may get the first turn of it.

"What a dark night!" said the colonel, as they came to the bottom of the hill, below Lark's cot; "perhaps we have met the moorland air. I never understand about such things, though I ought to do so thoroughly. It seems to me, to come in through the glass, a great deal more than the rain did. But perhaps I ought to lay the blame on my old eyes. Jack must have cats' eyes, to keep out of the ditch."

"I am sure he has very nice eyes, Colonel Westcombe; not at all like cats' eyes. And we ought to be very thankful to him, for the care he has taken of us all to-night."

"You seem to like Jack very much," said the colonel; though he felt, that it was not at all the thing to say.

"I never saw any one I liked more, as a stranger, of course, and a gentleman; unless it was yourself, Colonel Westcombe."

That gentleman thanked her, and said no more. Only to himself he thought—"Jack has still got his work to do; if he means to have this lovely girl. She respects him; but she does not love him yet. No girl, worth having, tumbles into deep affection, even for such a fine fellow as my son. He must have opportunities; and he shall have them, if her father is worthy to be her father. And I ought to find that out at once."

To his great chagrin, and the pure delight of Rose, who was thinking mainly of her father still, the densest depth of night, that ever drove down from Dartmoor, came around them. The rain stopped suddenly, and the wind was hushed, except in the tops of invisible trees; and a streak of black boggy fog settled heavily. The carriage-lamps (which had long been flickering, but managed to survive, while they got air) now gave up the ghost, in the murky reek.

"I can't see where to stop," Jack called in, through the front glass of the carriage. "I'm afraid that we must have passed the gate. Please to ask Miss Arthur."

"Please to stop here, if you have got my daughter," a clear voice, from one unseen, replied; and the panting horses, with their superior sense, came to a standstill suddenly.

"You shall not get out, Colonel Westcombe; I beg of you, for my sake, not to get out," cried Rose, that her father might know who was come. "Oh, father dear, how you must have been frightened! I will never go away again."

Jack Westcombe heard kissing, which went to his heart, as Rose sprang into her father's arms; and then Mr. Arthur, forgetful of everything, except the duty of a gentleman, came forward to the carriage-door, and said—

"Colonel Westcombe, I thank you, with all my heart for your great kindness to my child. Will you come into my cottage, and have something? You have many miles, I fear, to travel yet."

"Sir, I am very much obliged to you," the ancient officer answered, without even trying to descry the other's face, of which the darkness gave small chance; "but we must not stop, now we have done our duty. And a pleasure too,—the very greatest pleasure, to have been of the smallest service to a young lady, who has charmed me so. Good night, sir. Good night, my dear Miss Arthur. I only hope, that you have not caught cold."

"Oh, I do like him so much," said Rose, as the carriage rumbled down the hill; "he reminds me continually of you, papa. I do believe, you must have been a great deal together."

"It can hardly be possible," thought the colonel to himself; "and yet, I seemed to know the voice so well. But if so, poor fellow, how he is to be pitied! I scarcely know, what will be the proper thing to do."

CHAPTER VI.

THE vicar of Christowell, all this time, though he entered into society—as the people, who like to be from home, express it—was not unmindful of his wrongs. He had the pusillanimous feeling of a fellow, who objects to the wrong end of the stick; which now is received by our noble country, with a sweet request for more. The latter, no doubt, is the loftier way of getting the worst of it, and leads up to the surety of getting it again. However, the old style seems to have been, to lay hold of the cudgel, after serious groanings, and try how it would work, with the other end.

It was not any very low desire for redress, nor even that selfish sense of property, which now is being exploded by the powers of the age; nay, nor even that stability to dinner-time, which is now lost, because there is neither time

nor dinner—but it was a larger thing, which
bound the parson fast—as his own Mrs. Aggett
had been tied that day, to the steadfast right-
ing of his wrongs.

"Bain't no good for 'e, to prache to me," old
Betty Sage had declared to Mr. Short, when
he could not help calling her to account for
language, because of a baby running in between
her legs, when the day was warm, and she
was rather short of breath. "Passon Shart,
tend thee own ouze, fust. Happen, you swared
a bit, when they robbed 'e. Goo, and vaind
'un out, if 'e knooeth Holy Scripter."

It was not her opinion only (although it
carried great weight in the parish, now that
her husband was away, and believed to be
earning twice as much as he was worth) but
it was the universal sense concerning the
parson, and the sad way in which his people
touched their hats to him, and the heap of
small condolence which came in through Mrs.
Aggett, that really drove this very clever-
minded man, to try to do something that should
set him up again. For he could not bear to be
pitied, and advised, and to get no stick-thumps
on the floor, for the shrewd hits, and "prime
doctorin'," of the oldest, and wisest, of all his
sermons.

For the better preservation of the peace, an Act had been passed, in the very last session, and already was beginning to do a good deal of mischief, no further off than Exeter. A very considerable quantity of men had been appointed to preserve the peace, as " county, or district constables ;" but preferring foreign words to English, and knowing the fear that springs of them, they began to call themselves " Rural Police." Christowell had not heard of them yet, except through Carrier Pugsley ; but there was a man at Manaton, a superior parish constable, who said that he knew all about them, and could swear that they were the biggest fools going in the county.

Mr. Short, though he could not foresee the rising incapacity of this force, resolved (as a hater of new-fangled ways) to make no appeal to their vigilance. In his own shrewd mind, he had formed a firm belief, though without any premises producible, that the man, who had robbed his house, was no other than the rogue in the swamp, who had fired at his *Nous*. The people of the village,—though they tried to recollect, with a jogging of one memory against another,—could not be sure that they had seen anybody, in the very heavy rain, going by that day; though they thought they must have looked at him, if they had, because he would have been so wet-like. But without twice moving of their minds, they spied the sense of it. The One that jumped to the top of church-tower, the same came down to vicarage; both praying, and preaching, was an empty gun-shot, if you couldn't keep him out of your own kitchen.

"Physician, heal thyself," is the hardest, and most unanswerable of all taunts—in the present condition of medicine—and when it is proved against the parson of a parish, that he cannot keep the Prince of evil out of his own house, the sphere of his usefulness—to put it in the mildest form possible—becomes restricted. Parson Short was bound to be the master of his parish; and he vowed a great vow, not to give away sixpence, until his flock should be as dutiful as ever, and proud to run a race, when he whistled.

There was a little woman now, living at Okehampton, who knew everything about almost everybody. She was closely connected with literature, not only because she kept a little paper-shop, but also that she had a female cousin who wrote verses, and some of them were printed. The verses were good, and in the style of Dr. Watts, a poet under-valued now, almost as much as he is misquoted. But that is quite beside the present question. Only that some people took it on themselves, to declare that Mrs. Petherick never could have known all she did, except for her connection with the press, and her son being prenticed at Exeter.

" The women are a hundred times sharper than the men, round our part of the country," Jack Westcombe had said to Mr. Short, one day. " The men see things, and think no more about them; but they generally tell them to the women, at the time; and the women make the meaning out of them. The next time you come our way, go, and buy something from little Mrs. Petherick. You need not make her talk. She will do it, without asking; and you may pick something up, for she knows every-body. Don't tell her, who you are; see how cleverly she will find out."

The vicar had already made some expeditions into the depth of the moorland, and among the lonely farm-houses on the outskirts, in the vain hope of finding some trace of the fellow, who had carried off his money, and what he valued more, the watch of his respected grand-sire. Sometimes he took a fishing-rod, some-times a gun, as a pretext for his wanderings; and once or twice he rode, and fastened up his horse, while he was exploring dangerous parts. He even called once at the *Raven*, and saw the man who could have told him many in-teresting things; but Gruff Howell held his peace; and neither there nor elsewhere, was any sign forthcoming of the enemy. So now he went to see Mrs. Petherick, without even calling at Westcombe Hall.

The leaders of the age, whose main desire is to give fair play to every one, but first and foremost to all rogues,—as they perpetually prove, by preferring foreign to British produce—had lately made a mighty step towards en-lightenment, and adulteration—a march of in-tellect, known to the present generation, as the " Reform Bill." Although from a bill, it un-grubbed itself into an Act, and went hovering about, without doing half the harm expected (as a cock-chafer, after his larva stage, is harm-less, and amuses bad boys, when he is stuck upon a pin), yet there was a sad piece of mis-chief done here, in the very town where Mrs. Petherick lived. That ancient, and honourable town, Okehampton, baronial, royal-chartered, standing on two rivers, was found to contain such a scarcity of rogues, that it must not send any up to Parliament.

This blow had killed Mr. Petherick, according to the evidence of his widow, who must know best about it. He had always taken the lead, among one hundred and fifty freemen, who returned two members, with the truest pleasure, every time they required returning. There could be no meaner thing, than to dream of any possibility of harm in this. However, it must have been dreamed of; or why should Mrs. Petherick (who used to wear her own lace, on nomination-day, and again at the chairing, in her own bow-window) be driven, at the present time, to sell papers—though papers were a very decent trade, as yet—and spectacles, and tea-spoons of best Britannia metal, and to keep three young women in the back parlour, making lace to pattern for the ladies all around ?

Mr. Short knew very little of Okehampton, and was pleased to see how nice it looked, with its quiet old windows, and round-pebbled street, and church peeping down upon it from a wooded crest, and another church bravely send-

ing back the look; and above all, two very
tidy bridges, scarcely half a pipeful of tobacco
apart. Leisurely, and round-faced, folk live
here, with a large amount of female fatness,
and a breadth of brogue so spacious, that even
a Devonshire man can hardly make out, what
the boys are holloaing to one another. They
all said, " Sarvant, sir," to Mr. Short, as soon
as they had seen his horse, and white tie; for
the coaches, then running through the town
from Falmouth, had a tendency to import good
manners; wherein the railways do an export
trade alone. Sturdy urchins, vying with one
another, without any dream of a halfpenny for
guerdon, led Mr. Short to Mrs. Petherick's
shop; while *Trumpeter* stopped at the White
Hart, considering the important subject of
refreshment.

If Mrs. Petherick had a fault (besides the
original one of curiosity, which standeth in the
following of Eve) it was that she preferred a
new customer to an old one, being taken with
the beauty of the bird in the bush. In the
present loose days of co-operative stores (when
the noble mind hesitates, betwixt the pang of
paying twice too much for a thing, and the
pain of aggrieving a fine neighbourly spirit) it

may be true wisdom in a solid tradesman, to
flit about after fickle winds of money, because
he has no sure trade-wind. But forty years
ago, a hap-hazard shilling might cool itself on
the counter, while the books were being done.

"And what can I do for you sir, now? It
is a pleasure to see a new face in Okehampton;
the breeze of our wind brings a beautiful colour
into the cheeks of our visitors. I hope you
are come, to make a long stay, sir. The change
of the weather makes such a difference, don't
it? The clergy ought to go, for change of
air more often. Surely I must have the pleasure
of seeing the Rev. Brown, of Manaton?"

"I heartily hope that you may, Mrs. Pèthe-
rick," Mr. Short answered, without surprise,
being used to the style of the Devon shop-
keepers; "but I fear that you will have to wait
some time; for he is in the hands of three
doctors now."

"Ah, poor dear! It is very hard upon him.
What a wicked thing that gout is, to be sure!
It always attacks the clergy so bad! And
what a lovely set of lace, I sold him; perhaps
you have seen it upon Mrs. Brown, sir? Necklet,
with lappets down to here, and cuffs to match,
and a wide turn-over; all of the finest Honiton!

And then the lady wanted more; and I made sure that you was come about it. But what can I do for your good lady, sir? Eliza, bring me drawer No. 3. We have just done a set, of new Shinyoister pattern, the fashionable flower at the young Queen's court, all drawed first on tissue-paper, and improved by my own hand, sir."

"They are indeed beautiful;" said Mr. Short; "How I envy your taste, Mrs. Petherick! But alas, at present, there is no Mrs.—— Ah, there, I was going to be rude, and trouble you with my name; which would not interest you."

"Yes, indeed, it would, sir, very much. Sometimes it appears to me very hard, that we poor shop-keepers should be bound to keep our own names, over the door, and yet have no idea, who rings the bell. Did it ever strike you, in that light, sir?"

"Never, till now. But I at once confess the grievance. But oh, Mrs. Petherick, you know too much already! I hear that you are the cleverest lady, in Okehampton."

"Only in the way of laces, sir, and book-learning, and politeness. There are many as can buy, and sell me; because what they sell is downright rubbish. I just get the cost of the thread, and the time, and the victuals my

young ladies eats.   You may see them at work,
if you come here.   They like to be looked at by
a gentleman ; but away go their pillows, if a
lady peeps in."

"Come, come, Mrs. Petherick, you are too
bad. I did not mean to buy any lace. But
have you any pattern in roses? I know a
young lady—quite a child——"

" Then, sir, I have the very thing for you.
Moss-roses in the bud, my own designing ; the
loveliest thing, and so reasonable ! "

The parson bought a very pretty piece of
work, for a couple of guineas, and was having it
packed, when the coach from Falmouth, the old
Defiance, came over the western bridge at a
brisk trot, with a great horn-blowing, and
pulled up at the inn. Mrs. Petherick rushed
to the window to gaze, and her customer opened
the door, to do the same.

"My goodness, there he is ! I shall drop;
sir, I shall drop," the little woman cried; but
she did not drop, though her ruddy cheeks lost
all their colour.   " What a burning shame it is
to our country, that such a villain should walk
the earth ! "

Mr. Short, without asking what she meant,
stepped back, to be sure that she did not want

help; and then, instead of going to the door
again, took a chair, and sat down to watch the
coach, through the light things hanging in the
window. There was nothing unusual, so far as
he could see. The coachman did what a coachman always does, or did until he became
extinct. He threw down the reins, with a condescending nod, handed his whip to a gentleman behind—for the gentleman on the box
descended to stand treat—and then after thumping himself on the chest, although it was a
shirt-sleeve day, down he went, very clumsily
and slowly, even as a boatman is one of the
worst to get into, or out of, his own boat.

"He is a most abstemious man," said Mrs.
Petherick; "at this time of year, he scarcely
ever takes anything stronger than brandy and
lemonade. That man has fourteen children.
And he scarcely looks five and thirty yet. He
is planting his children all along the road. He
drives twelve stages, up one day, and down the
next; and they say that he means to have two
children at every stage, all born in holy matrimony; as I myself can testify, because his wife
was a barmaid here." The lady of the shop
had now recovered from her scare, and seemed
anxious to divert attention from it. But the
parson would not have it so.

" If I may ask, without rudeness," he said,
" what was it that frightened you, when the
coach came in ? They all seem very quiet, tidy
people. My sight is pretty good. I can see
their faces ; and I cannot see anything formidable
yet. Perhaps, the one that frightened you
jumped down, before I looked."

" No, sir, he is there with his shoulders
towards us, and his back against a brown-haired
trunk. These day-coaches carry no proper
guard ; they only have a boy to blow the horn ;
and the man I mean is sitting, or slouching,
next to the one who is opposite the boy. There,
he has put his hand up to his chin ! "

The street is of a good width in that part,
and the coach having stopped some little way
back, as well as on the other side, and having
luggage on the roof, the hind passengers could
not be discerned very clearly, from the window
of the paper shop. And the man with his hand
to his chin appeared to be sleepy, and scornful
perhaps of the town ; so that he did not turn
round, and stare about.

" You will see him better presently, when
they come by ; but you had better not seem to
notice him," Mrs. Petherick continued, as she
hung a scarf across, to baffle any eyes that

might invade her. "I would not let him see me, not for £50; to know, I mean, that I was watching him. Sometimes I have lace to repair for ladies, worth £200 or more; let alone ten, or twelve, drawerfuls of my own."

"But surely, my dear madam, you never mean to say, that a man would be riding about on a coach, in broad daylight, who would break in, and steal your lace!"

"Not lace in particular, sir, but anything. Nothing comes amiss to him; and he can break in, anywhere. And as for his riding on the coach, there is no one, in the town or out of it, who would know him, in the manner he is dressed up now; or if they did, they would not dare. He is quite the gentleman, when he chooses; and he got some very good clothes, no doubt, when he plundered that stupid Parson Short."

"What Parson Short?" asked the parson of that name; "there are several in the diocese, I believe."

"The rich Parson Short, sir, of Christowell. I am told, it was a most amusing thing. He was lured from home, like a simple Simon; and when he come back, he found his cook tied up, and all his dinner eaten, and the other maid locked in, with no other food than his sermons, for the day. And I hear that she found them uncommon tough, and dry. No wonder, poor girl, for he is the very dryest man that ever went up the pulpit-stairs. Our people did laugh, when they heard the joke. And they say, that he boiled the parson's spinach, for he is a bit of an epicure, you must know, and was going to have it with a breast of lamb; but the other man enjoyed it, and then fastened up the dish, over the face of the poor fat cook. But the other man had his disappointment too; for the gentleman's leg-garments would not come below his knee. Short by name, he is, and short by nature."

He was almost short in language too; and his clear and clean face flushed with wrath, at this stinging description of his woes.

"This must be a most outrageous town for gossip," he said, looking sternly at the streets thereof; "and full of wicked falsehoods, and very low ones."

"No, sir, not more than anywhere else," Mrs. Petherick answered pleasantly; "but we do love a pretty tale about a clergyman; and every word of what I have been telling you is true. But here they are off, with a flourish of the whip. Now, if you will look between that paper and the tambour-work, you will have a good view of the gentleman that did it. Shall I tell you, what he has been to Falmouth for?"

"I know that some parts of your story are wrong, and I doubt whether you know anything about it." He spoke a little rudely, to provoke her tongue, while he watched for that felonious passenger.

"No, sir, you are quite right. I don't know an atom about him. I don't know the figure, how he holds himself, whatever clothes he may put on, nor the individdle way of making lines inside his clothes, that the men get, by reason of no stiffness. And perhaps I don't know why he went to Falmouth, to get the best price for a celebrated watch, such as they can work a ship by. I did hear that it was worth £200. But I don't know, I am sure; I don't know anything."

"It is the man!" cried Mr. Short, as the coach passed slowly, with laborious wind of horn; "I can't tell how I know it; but I am sure that he is the man. What makes him come through the town, like this, when he might have got down, four or five miles back? And how far will he go with the coach? Mrs.

Petherick, you seem to me to know everything."

"No, sir, no. I make no pretences. But to
my humble thinking, he has come through the
town, because it was the safest thing for him
to do. His pockets are full of money; and a
robber is always most frightened of being
robbed. There is a gang of louters, Sourton
way, who would cry shares with him, if they
spied him in his clericals. And as for the
danger of the town, there is none. We have a
man, who calls himself a constable; but he
never stirs without a warrant; and we have a
very nice old gentleman indeed, just made a
Justice of the Peace; but all he can do is to
fight the battle of Waterloo, or Salamander,
again. And as for the mayor, he won't do
nothing, ever since we were robbed of our old
borough. The whole of the difference between
right, and wrong, was upset, when they took
away both members."

"What is a lobster worth, without his claws?
But how far will this clerical gentleman go,
after riding in triumph through Okehampton?"

"As far as Crosscombe, sir, most likely, and
then take the lane to Sticklepath, or Belstone.
That will bring him back to the wild parts

of the moor, by an easier way than Sourton. And he shifts about pretty often, I believe; though he is more at home than welcome, as we say, whatever part he lives in. But good heart alive, you are never going after him! You would be a baby, in his hands."

"Babies are troublesome creatures sometimes," exclaimed Mr. Short, being vexed once more; "but I am not going after him, with any idea of laying hands on him, among a lot of cowards; when he has fire-arms, and I have none. I beg you to make no stir about it; for that would defeat my object. Do not even see me, when I get my horse out. I am Mr. Short, of Christowell, whose dryness in the pulpit is proverbial here, though quite satisfactory to his own parish. It is not true, that yonder fellow ate my dinner; but still I have a bone to pick with him; and my chance will be spoiled, if you talk about it. I thank you for your very shrewd hit about my watch. The cleverest woman in the town should be so far superior to her sex, that she can hold her tongue, when a great pinch is put on it."

"The only difficulty that I find is, to express myself, not to contain myself, sir. When poor Petherick was paying of them freemen, average of £15 per vote, and the other side was trying every low inducement—— "

" Another time, if you please, I shall be delighted. I want the old *Defiance* to get well in front; and I don't want to seem to be riding in chase. It is a long hill towards Cross-combe, and stirrups will easily beat traces. Now if you say nothing about this affair, I will not even tell my old friend Colonel Westcombe, to fight his battles over again with me."

" You have read me a lesson, to be shy of the clergy, sir. They always looks, as if they was so gracious; and then they drop on you, like the core of a box-oven. But you had better not take your lace, sir."

" No; I will pay for it, and ask you to send it to kind care of Colonel Westcombe. I hope to be there, in a day or two. Good-bye, ma'am."

" Good-bye, sir. I need not tell you, I think, to take care of yourself; you are sure to do that. It would take a sharp man to eat his dinner"— she continued to herself, as she beheld him crossing the street, without any sign of hurry, to get his horse out of the stable. " Short he may be; and no wonder

he was short with me, after what I said of
him ; but the short men are the best to wrestle,
after all. Why there he goes, horse and all!
The Lord deliver him!"

Mr. Short however required no especial de-
liverance, on this occasion. At a mile, or so,
over East Ockment bridge, he sighted the
Defiance on the crown of a hill, and his keen
eyes showed him, that the interesting passenger
was sitting in the same place on the roof.
Then he followed very cautiously, and kept
behind the corners, until the coach stopped,
where a narrow lane departed, on the right
hand side, towards Belstone, and the moor.
Here he saw the tall man get down, and pay
his fare, and swing a little knapsack on his
shoulder, containing perhaps some good things
from Falmouth. Then the villain looked about,
to be sure that no one watched him, and presently set off along the narrow lane, with the
top of his hat showing over the dry wall.
Short rode into a gateway of the turnpike-
road, and considered that hat, as it jogged
along the loopholes of the granite slabs.

"I could cut him off easily enough," he
thought; "and call him to account; but he
would settle me. He is sure to have at least

one tremendous pistol; and I have nothing
but this hunting-crop. It would have been
foolish to attack him on the coach; for nobody
would have helped me, and there were two
women there. It would be still more foolish
to attack him now, without even a witness to
my murder. After all, that is not my hat. It
is much too respectable to belong to me. He
bought it at Falmouth with my money. Perhaps, I am a coward; but why should a good
man be killed for nothing? What would Mrs.
Aggett say? And who would carry on all
my works? Nay, I will be discreet, and only
observe him beyond bullet-range. If I accosted
him, as a neutral, it would do more harm than
good; as I know him already, and he then
would know me, which is not at all to be
desired.

With these reflections, he restrained himself,
as a truly wise man is bound to do; and calmly
postponing the settlement of accounts, resolved
to help it one line forward, by observing the
route of the enemy. Therefore, as soon as he
came to a gate, where the rocky expanse of the
desert began, he fastened up his horse, and
going warily afoot, had the pleasure of descry-
ing a dark figure in the distance, and watching

it follow the desolate windings of Belstone
Cleeve, towards the source of the Skate river.
Here a three-knuckled hill, with water-clefts,
and yellow knolls of rushes, and swamp-reeds,
barred the view; and the distant form disappeared among them, after turning to the right.

"He has made for Cranmere. It is about
a league further. None but the moormen could
find him there. It is hard enough to find the
place itself, much more such an atom as a man,
among it. Well, well, I have done something;
and as much as I could hope to do. *Trumpeter*
must be quite tired of waiting. Suppose we
go quietly home to dinner, with gratitude, and
a fine appetite."

CHAPTER VII.

PEOPLE of so bald a nature, as to find but little joy in all the things around them, take at any rate some delight in their own superior thickness. With pleasure, they look down upon the fads, the crotchets, and the hobbies, of the few who still have soft enjoyment, outside money, and away from show. Yet these latter smile at laughter; and the smile outlives the louder operation; even as the sun survives the storm.

Every just man has his periods for incurring the opinions of the wiseacres, when his name turns up, through a law-suit, or an accident, or perhaps some great wrong done to him. And his true course is to exclude all care, not only as to what those wiseacres say, but whether they even draw their fleeting breath about him. And after short disquietude, and a little counsel with himself, Mr. Arthur resolved to follow this true course. His friend, Mr. Short, would have done the very same, in his own case, if possible. But he, as a clergyman, must not suffer fools to undermine his influence.

Fearing to have brought upon her father, not only unpleasant recollection, but sad perplexities imminent, Rose Arthur was delighted to find him as cheerful as usual, on the following day. He listened, with interest and amusement, to the thousand and one things she had to tell, about her first great party; and he said, that he hoped it would not be very long, before she had another little change, to make her lively.

"No, papa, no; I want no more, for a very, very long time indeed," she answered; "and I was so vexed at what happened last night, because—because I know, that you dislike to be disturbed so."

"It was no disturbance, my dear child. I am glad, upon the whole, that it has happened so. Colonel Westcombe was most kind to you; and I wish that I could thank him better. But I do not in the least expect, that he will ever come again."

He said this with a smile, which seemed to Rose a very sad one. And she was grieved,

more than she liked to show, at such a conclusion to her sudden friendship, though she
would not ask, why it must be so.

" There are reasons, which I cannot explain
to you, my dear," Mr. Arthur continued, as
he understood her glance, "which prevent me
from having any intercourse with the man,
whom of all in this part of the world, and I
may even say in the entire world, I respect,
and admire, and like the best. If circumstances should entirely change, or even without that, if I should be taken with dangerous illness, it would become my duty to
explain everything to you; or if I should be
taken from you suddenly, all the particulars
will be found in writing, as I have told you,
once or twice. Now, for the work of the day,
my darling. Busy hands make happy minds.
The storm of last night has done good, upon
the whole, and the air is beautifully soft
to-day. But there must be a lot to do in the
little vineyard; and I think I must call upon
you to help. The wind is the worst foe the
vine has in this country; though the May-
frosts are worse than wind, in the east of
England. In any part of Southern England,
where those bitter May-frosts do not prevail,

it is my firm belief that, with proper care and skill, and experience as to the right sort to grow, a much finer table-grape can be got, out-of-doors, than you can buy in Germany, or the northern half of France; and for this simple reason, that——"

"Come, dear father, you like to deliver that lecture after supper. And you will be angry with yourself, and me too, if we stop to have it now—for it always lasts an hour—when we ought to be hard at work, in Naboth's vine-yard. It is the first time you have ever had the manners to invite me, to do a bit of work there—you are so jealous! I quite understand it. There are plants of mine, that you dare not touch, in your most audacious moment. However, I will go and get my 'tuck-ups,' as you call them, and overtake you in two seconds. But what am I to sit upon—the ground?"

"Never mind about that. There are flower-pots there, that your stupid Pugsley brought, only fit to sit upon; and some of them kick up, even so. There never was a pot of sense, till I invented mine, and had them made. And even, after that, the clay was so inferior, and they were kilned in such a doltish manner——"

The rest of this lamentation passed out of

hearing, as the puffs of the captain's pipe flitted through the bright air, while he was marching away among his pear-trees, and glancing at the increase of their hopes. The fresh remembrance of the rain was on them, sparkling still from some cupped leaf; and the new shoots of summer were embrowning slowly their thick sappy green, into the dignity of rind. In sturdy little sheaves, were the young pears standing, with the setting of their eyes pricked up like cloves, and the bronzing of the sun, and air, shed round their sides already. Others, of the long curved stalk, and pensive habit, hung their heads, with paler tints generally, and more grey upon their oval drops.

Thankful as a gardener is, at the prospect of a noble crop, he is anxious also that it should not fail, through failure of his grumbling. Right well he knows, through vast experience, what blows descend from heaven upon his first indulgence in a vaunt; and grateful as he is, beyond mankind, he humbly secretes his gratitude. " What a lot of thinning there will be to do ! We shall never get through it; " cried Mr. Arthur.

" Won't we, though ? I can do a score of trees before breakfast, any fine morning," his daughter answered, as she overtook him ; " and even you acknowledge, that I understand that work. We ought to be only too glad, to have to do it. But it goes to my heart, at every tap, to see the little darlings hopping on the ground. Now shall I go on to Jezreel, or begin it ? "

" I will not have my little nook called 'Naboth's Vineyard.' The confusion of ideas is too feminine. Am I, the owner, envious of my own ownership, because I shut out clumsy people ? The only analogy, that can be imagined, would set you down first as an Ahab."

" Very well, dear, if that will please you better, it shall be Solomon's Vineyard, such as he describes—I believe, somewhere. And I will be the Queen of Sheba, come to see it. Only you must have the manners, in that case, to provide me with at least a sound flower-pot, to sit upon, instead of one of your break-downs. And none of your sound ones have got anything to sit upon. Oh, papa, you are so clever, do invent something that is not all holes."

" The special virtue of my pots is this," Mr. Arthur stopped short, when he began upon that, although in a great hurry to get on ; " that they are all holes, or at any rate contrived so that you can tell, at a glance, what is

going on inside. There is. a very clever
Frenchman, of the name of Beaumont, who has
found a man endowed with a window in his
digestive organs, by means of a bullet, or a
grapeshot. He is thus enabled to ascertain—
but never mind, my dear, you are too young, as
yet, for inquiries of pure science. And I would
not have hinted at the—well I may call it, the
troublesome part of the human system—except
to elucidate my theory of pots. There are three
essential qualities in a flower-pot, to begin with;
and there are fifteen of less, but still important
consideration——"

"Her be coming, her be coming, at a rattle,"
Moggy, the maid, came hotly shouting; "shall
us let 'un in, or shall us shut 'un out?"

"Who is it, that causes you so much excitement, Moggy?" her master asked, with some
little vexation, for he was just warming up to
his subject, with the pleasure of the vines in
prospect; "I have no time to see any one."

"Her ladyship, Lady Tichwudd; I knowed
that bragian boy in front, as looketh daown on
his own kearful moother. No room for he, in
my kitchen. I was vorced to box the ears of
'un, last time."

"Do it again, if needful, Moggy. We will

go, and meet Lady Touchwood, at the gate. Her carriage cannot cross the stream. Come, Rose, and thank her for her kindness to you yesterday."

" Keep the horses exercised for one hour, and then be here again, to see if I am ready," Mr. Arthur, and his daughter, heard the order given, as they came back reluctantly to the draw-bridge, and beheld their visitor, with the page behind her, crossing the space between the river and the lane. " Ah, how pleased I am to see you ! " she exclaimed, as the captain lowered his plank, and politely led her across it ; " I scarcely expected such good luck. And darling Rose, how well you look ! It was very dull yesterday for you, I fear. But you would run away so. There was to have been a little dance, if the weather had only been propitious —what my son Richard will call a ' hop ; ' and then perhaps somebody would not have run away so, or at any rate, would not have been allowed the chance. I know one, who would have pleaded very hard ; and he generally manages to get his own way. How ingenious it was about all those fish ! I never saw so many, and how fresh they were ! And how wonderfully you did cook them, dear ! Canon

Botrys made a splendid joke, so Mrs. Botrys
herself told Julia, who between you and me,
captain, is a trifle jealous. The canon said,
' that young lady dresses fish, almost as well as
she dresses herself.' Not so very bad for a
dignitary of the Church. And he stuck to his
plate, till he got wet through. And then Julia,
who understands all the foreign tongues, said—
' give him some extra sec to dry him.' Upon
the whole, it was very pleasant, except for that
abominable rain. But I never heard how you
got home, my dear. You must not think it
remiss, on my part. All was such desperate
confusion, in the storm."

"Oh, I got home beautifully, Lady Touchwood. Colonel Westcombe brought Miss Perperaps to her own house; and then he brought
me to my father's gate."

"Oh, indeed! What a gallant old officer!
It seems to me that Colonel Westcombe does
almost everything. And I suppose, his son was
with him, too. A very polite young man, I
believe; though with very little to say for
himself."

" We did not want him to talk," Rose answered,
with a little flush of anger on her cheeks;
" what we wanted, or at least what he wanted,

was, to bring us safely through the dark stormy
night, and the dangerous roads, which he ventured on for our sake.   And he did it; though
he must have been half-blinded by the rain.
Very few people could have done it, I am
sure."

"My son is a noble whip, and he faces any
weather.   But I made him come inside; for he
is not of coarse fibre.   And even so, I fear, that
he has taken a sad cold.   Ever since that sad
calamity on your premises, he has caused me
great uneasiness.   Perhaps no other young man,
in the world, could have survived it.   But he is
of such elastic tissue, and unusual harmony of
juncture,—as an eminent medical authority pronounced, before he was breeched (I beg your
pardon for the word), that he seems to rise
superior to all trials."

"Let us hope, then," said Mr. Arthur very
kindly, "that he will soon throw off his cold.
Shall we go into my little sitting-room, which
cherishes a memory of pipes, I fear?   Or would
you like to rest a little, in my summer plant-
house, which is thrown open now, and has no
sun upon it?"

"No, if I may choose, I would rather be in
doors.   Under glass, I should have an expecta-

tion, every moment, of my son coming tumbling in upon me. And I do not object to the smell of tobacco. Sir Joseph, in his few angel-visits to the park, calls for his pipe immediately. And my beloved son tries very hard to do it. Such ideas consecrate a smell, however nasty."

"You prove again the well-known truth of the unselfishness of ladies," Mr. Arthur answered, with a smile more genial, than any he had yet vouchsafed her. For nothing but the stiffness of his manner, and the fence of distant courtesy, had kept this lady from breaking into the coveted circle of his own affairs. While, according to the laws of nature, she held him in tenfold esteem, and viewed him with a hundred-fold of interest, because she could not get at him; "but my Rosie sees that this room is well-aired; and the door into the greenhouse keeps it fresh."

"I call it charming—a lovely little room," Lady Touchwood declared, as she tied her parasol up; "and the flowers that come tapping, tapping, as somebody, perhaps Lord Byron, says. Julia loves him; but my son Richard, who has Grecian features, and should be a judge, pronounces his morality imperfect. However, I never read such subjects. What's the use of rhyme? We don't talk in rhyme; and it must take a dreadful lot of time to make it. Oh, I should so like to take that moss-rose to my son! May I ask your daughter to go, and cut it for me? We can't grow moss-roses, at Touchwood Park."

While Rose ran away on this little errand, the visitor told Mr. Arthur briefly, that she was come to speak about his dear child, and could not do it in her presence. So another commission was found for Rose, and she went about it gladly.

"You have thought it very strange of me, to come so early," the visitor resumed, when the coast was clear, "but oh, Captain Arthur, you can make allowance for the deep anxieties of a mother. Tired as I was, after all the fag of yesterday—for, in simple truth, those parties are a dreadful plague—not a wink of sleep could I get last night, with perpetual worry about my darling boy. He never used to know his own mind at all; and that was so delightful of him. But now, I fear that his heart is fixed irretrievably, irre—something, I never can remember those big words, something like bad play at whist."

"Irrevocably, perhaps?" asked the captain

with a bow; "but, excuse me, perhaps that is not the word."

"That is the word to a nicety, and I suppose there is no English for it. Irrevocably fixed his poor young heart is, upon your very charming daughter. Now, don't say a word until I have finished; and then we shall understand each other. I could have wished it otherwise, as I need hardly say; although I confess it would be difficult to find a nicer, a more charming; a more lady-like young lady. Her behaviour yesterday was simply perfect; for she scarcely said anything, and all she did was useful. Many of the very highest people were quite captivated with her. What a sweet, pretty thing she had got on! I am sure it must have been made in Paris. My daughter Julia was quite put out; and it pleased me to see, how well she bore it."

"Excuse my saying that Miss Touchwood, in her style, is above all possibility of rivalry." Mr. Arthur felt that politeness called for this, after all those gratifying praises of his daughter.

"No doubt, that was her own opinion. Julia never under-rates herself; as my son Richard always does. People make a great mistake, on that account. They positively think that my son Richard is below the average of intellect. Because he is modest, and conceals his gifts, he is supposed not to have them. But how could he conceal them, if he had not got them? Now that is sound reasoning, as you must perceive. Even Mr. Short, with all his chatter about logic, could never get out of such an argument as that. Yet people keep on saying, that we ladies cannot argue!"

"There can be no greater mistake," replied the captain; "it should rather be said, that ladies can argue always."

"I am so glad that you agree with me, because it saves so much reasoning; and excitement does not suit me now. I consider you infinitely superior, in the style of your mind, to Mr. Short; who has the nastiest way of putting things. And I have always found the military far more reasonable than the clericals. Now, you have been an officer, haven't you, Captain?"

"Well!" said Mr. Arthur, who could not help smiling, for the turn was sudden, even for a lady; "it would be very unpolite on my part, to decline a lady's commission."

"It is not curiosity that makes me ask, nor any inferior sentiment; but a lofty sense of duty only.   The daughter of an officer, whether he has fought for his country, or whether he has been more fortunate, stands upon a social level, which—which is very excusable, for any rank to fall in love with her.   But Captain Arthur, if this is to go on, you would, I trust, leave off gardening.   It is a very amiable peculiarity, especially if you lose money by it; which elevates it above trade, and makes it quite respectable.   You must not feel hurt, at my expressions, but to have your name upon a basket—what would the county families say?"

"I have not considered the subject yet, from that point of view, which is a new one to me. But would the county families pay for all I should lose, in the way of wicker-work?"

"I fear not; for they are dreadful screws. They sell their grapes, and pine-apples, but they object to the appearance of their names.   However, you might have a private mark, a star, or a lion, or your family crest; so we might get over that objection.   But you must come out of your retirement, Captain Arthur; your seclusion, I might even call it.   You must resume your rank, and visit people."

"Lady Touchwood, you mean well, and kindly.   And I am bound to hear, what you

have to say, not only with courtesy due to a
lady, but also with some gratitude. For you
have not touched on one point, which would
have been the foremost, with many ladies
placed as you are. You have not spoken of
my poverty. Of that I am not ashamed—for
no one need be—still it is kind of you, not to
refer to the difference in worldly goods between
us; and for that, I respect, and like you. And
that makes it far more difficult for me to say,
what I must say, before we understand each
other."

"If it is anything about—about any mis-
understanding, between you and the law, surely
we can get it put to rights. Sir Joseph has
such influence, in the very highest quarters."

"No, there is nothing of that kind," he
replied, with a smile that was perfectly con-
vincing; "I have never done anything felonious. My seclusion is of my own seeking.
What I have to say, is about your son, who is
a most amiable, and lively youth. He brought
a new spirit into our dull round; and we all
missed him greatly, when he left us. But if
there were no other obstacles, although, as you
clearly see, there are plenty, there is a fatal
one at the outset. The character of your son

is not formed yet. He is volatile, versatile, clever in his way; but a perfect boy, at present."

"That is exactly what his father says," Lady Touchwood answered, with unwonted self-control; "but youth is a fault that will right itself. You will not condemn him, on that account."

"It is a fault that should right itself, before marriage, and even before an engagement is formed," Mr. Arthur said decisively; "unless the lady is of strong commanding spirit, and can shape her lord. My little Rosie is gentle, sensitive, warm-hearted, loving, and impetuous sometimes, but never inclined to be imperative. She is wholly unsuitable for your son."

"Then am I to understand, Mr. Arthur, that you decline to have anything to do with my Dicky?"

"By no means; I am always glad to see him; and indeed I have a hunt in view for him. But concerning of my daughter, as the people say here, it is not to be thought of; and I can trust her."

Lady Touchwood looked at him, with anger in her eyes, and the vertical lines of temper, on her forehead, deepening into a puzzle of dismay. She wanted to say the rudest thing that she could think of, and cast about for it, and would have found it, if the eyes of her antagonist had either flashed, or wavered. But the captain regarded her, from his superior height, with a gaze of good will, not only philosophical, but of the very finest breeding. "He must be somebody. Perhaps he is a lord! He would jump at Dicky, unless he was a lord," were the ponderings of her mind, which made her humble.

"I am sure, Captain Arthur, that you mean it for the best." She relapsed, from the baffled issue of great wrath, into the common-place, as hot people do. "You are the best judge upon such matters. You have seen a vast deal of the world, that is certain, from the common sense, of what you say. Nobody gets common sense, without it. I am disappointed. I can say no more. My son is an exceedingly interesting young man; and hitherto nobody has been able to resist him. He is so much accustomed to have his own way; this will be a bitter blow to him."

"And it will do him good, a weight of good, a world of good. You will have cause to be glad of this little check to his rapidity. Ladies have such sympathy with love-affairs, that they scarcely ask how they will react upon themselves. If your son were engaged, before he is a man, what peace would you ever have with him? Every day, he would vow to be married to-morrow."

"That is true enough," said Lady Touchwood. "How you have understood his brave nature!'

"Then, if you let him marry, what would come of it? His bride would be everything, while she was a bride; and he would even be rude to his dear mother. Let him wait, ten years, Lady Touchwood; and he will be a man by that time; or at any rate, he ought to be."

"Your advice is excellent," the lady answered; for some of her tenderest feelings had been touched. "Dicky is already very difficult to manage. And if he had a wife to encourage him, my condition would be dreadful, as you say. I quite agree with you, that he should wait for many years. But I have such a dread of his being entangled by some objectionable person; and he turns up his nose against girls with money. There is a most charming girl, Chrysolite Moneywig; not half so nice as your daughter, I admit, because she is captious, and conceited, and a prig, and thinks too much of literature, and she dresses according to the poets always; which is the most absurd thing, with a hundred thousand pounds. However, I could keep her down, no doubt: because she must be a foolish thing. But Dicky is afraid of her; and she won't have him, unless he should happen to be senior wrangler. And he doesn't seem to care to be that sort of thing."

"Never mind; let him act according to his lights," Mr. Arthur answered, with a cheerful smile. "You are happy in having a son, Lady Touchwood, who is healthy, active, and easily pleased, and as frank as the day, about everything. Such natures are happiest in the long run; for they seldom fall into great depth of trouble. He will soon get over this, and be as bright as ever."

"But will you break it to him? He has been so plaguesome. Yesterday something made him frightfully jealous. And you have more influence with him, than any one. He always speaks of you so highly."

"Certainly, I will; if you wish me to do so. I will be gentle with him; as I need not tell you. And it is better to act at once, decisively."

With this understanding, Lady Touchwood left, feeling more good will towards Mr. Arthur, than could have been expected in so delicate a case.

CHAPTER VIII.

PERILOUS ENTERPRISE.

WHENEVER a thing begins to move, it is wonderful how it will go on. There was a man
in Devonshire, who lay in bed, as his own wife
said of him, for one and twenty years, with
no other reason than because he liked it, and
found his constitution thrive. He enjoyed a
pension, from the British crown, of twelve
shillings a week, paid quarterly; because his
father—much against his own desire—had received a bullet intended for a member of the
royal family. It appears, that the fate of
the parent dwelled, with singular force, upon the
filial mind; and the son reasoned justly, that
as his dear father had brought on his decease,
by standing up, he of the next generation
might avoid the like result, by lying down. It
is impossible to penetrate into the human mind;
and this man's motive, or determination not

to move, may have been even larger. However, there he was for thrice seven years; and the neighbourhood respected him, because he did no work. And he might have been there now, if he had only stuck fast. But there came a new curate, of uneasy mind, who fancied that this man was neglecting duty, and who would rouse him up to a sense of his position. He made him get half-way up at first, and look out of the window, and see the river; and with six months of energy, he stirred him up into his breeches, which were hanging on a peg by the door; like mildewed stirrups, when the horse is dead. Even a pensioner may thus be killed. The poor fellow saw the churchyard, from a window going downstairs, and shook his head; for he preferred a pillow to a tombstone. For a few days, he exerted some reluctant steps, and then became a walking funeral.

So it is also with the rest of us, who must get out of bed, because we have no pension. When once we get out of the tranquil horizontal, into the whirl of the vertical state, we are hurrying ourselves, very much against our own desires, to a larger world. Neither is that, however bad it may be, by any means the worst of it.

For we have provoked, into a restless mood, things that are only too glad to have some excuse, for not standing still on us. With sudden alacrity, they begin to slide; and like sticks in an avalanche, we go too.

The perception of this great truth was clearer, in the ancient times, than it is to-day. We find it consistently impressed upon us, by the chorus in Greek plays, by Pindar also, and the wise Theognis, and the genial Herodotus. Hence, with flowing weight, it descends into the grand lines of Lucretius, the torrent of Catullus, and the sudden turns of Horace. And there used to be plentiful sense of it with us, till loftier science took command of sense.

Now, Mr. George Gaston was a very able man, and one of great activity; therefore he laughed at the maxim of antiquity, *quieta noli movere;* which is, in our vernacular, " let sleeping dogs lie." He had roused up sleeping dogs, to make them follow him; and at first they seemed to do so, without troubling him to whistle. But before very long, they began to sniff about, and make little excursions on their own account.

In this man's arrogant inroad on Mr. Tucker, he had been guilty of the old mistake of supposing, that Devonshire people are thick-headed, with a thickness that leaves no space inside. It is not to be denied that their skulls are solid; but every melon-grower will maintain that the substance of his rind has its own advantage, and enhances the coolness of the choice contents. Therefore it would have been a more sagacious act on the part of Gaston, to have kept his temper, poured graceful praises on his host's glass drum-sticks, and cordially departed, with a hope to come again.

Not that this excellent old gentleman, retired from the timber-trade, fostered any twist of sap about it. His grain was good, and he would cut up well; and before he was cut up, or even cut down, he was a fine piece of maturity, and sound at core. The impertinence of his red-faced guest was gone from his mind, when he said his prayers, that night. And when it was brought up again, the next day, by some indignation of his sister, Mr. Tucker only said, that such a class of persons was below the contempt of right-minded people. And the only thing that acted on his mind at all, was a doubt whether it might be his duty, to write to the gentleman on Dartmoor, and tell him, that some low fellow was inquisitive about him. But doubting lets the time go by; and time went by, without a letter to deliver.

All this was according to the manner of mankind; who, when worthy of the name, cast off as a plaguesome burden, little enmities. But even as a man may kill his own queen-wasps, and bring in their bodies, and have them pitied; so, if he is too magnanimous to kill them, somebody will set forth, to do that duty for him, and probably it will be a lady.

Mrs. Giblets, and her daughter Mary, when they heard what the high-coloured man had said, and done, longed only to run after him, and pull him off his horse. But finding that he was gone too far, for any chance of laying hands on him, they consoled themselves with some fine old proverbs, whose pith was, that their time would come. And so it did, to their own great amazement; although they had been so confident about it. For it happened that the whilom Mayoress of Barum (whose Mary had been born into a silver cradle, as well as with a silver spoon in her mouth) possessed a sister of a wandering turn, who, after many ups and downs, had turned up well. That is to say, she had married a man for the third time—not the same man, of course; though such a thing has happened, in these cycles of divorce—and the third time was lucky, as it ought to be. Husband No. 3 made up for 1, and 2, who had gone to their rest at the public expense; for although he had entered on the matrimonial stage, with more courage than cash, he obtained his reward. He invested £5, on his very wedding-day, reasoning well that he could not be hit both ways; and only keeping fifteen shillings, for the outlay of the honeymoon. Fortune repaid his manly confidence so briskly, that his £5 turned into five and twenty, before he got his first uxorial wigging; that is to say, within three days. For that was the golden era of the railway rush, when even solid heads were spinning, and generally got the worst of it, in clashing with the light ones. In a few months, Mr. Snacks was worth more than five and twenty thousand pounds; then he got in his cash, invested in safe mortgages, which were almost going begging, bought a nice house near Regent's Park, and only kept a small amount in speculation.

Mrs. Snacks had always borne in mind the kindness of her brother, Mr. Tucker, and her sister, Mrs. Giblets; both of whom had helped her, to the best of their convenience, in the

bygone days of poverty. And now she longed
to make them some return, as well as to show
them her new house, and prove to Mr. Snacks
what she had always said—that she belonged
to a family, he might be proud of. Also there
was a little Snacks by this time, the first fruit
of the lady's triple conjunction, and he seemed
sometimes to languish for lack of admiration.
Neither was it utterly beyond the book of fate,
that some of the pleasant timber-merchant's
money might be directed, by a hospitable turn,
towards his godson, the junior Snacks. Mr.
Tucker however declined stage-coaching, and
could not bear the jolting of the rail beyond it;
which the driver of the *Quicksilver* declared
would kill a bull. His sister, being younger,
might attempt it, if she chose; and Mary could
never have enough see-saw. Therefore, these
two accepted invitations; and a swing was put
up in the old walnut-tree, to bring them into
training for the tossings of the line.

It must have been the middle of July, when
they were ready; and they all wept heartily,
when they said " good-bye." The travellers
took a cask of salted butter, three Devonshire
hams, and a round of spiced beef, and assert-
ing (to assure themselves) their confidence in

Heaven, set forth upon this enterprise of ambition, and audacity.

After many marvels, and a vast prolongation of their lives—if life, as is now contended, can be measured only by perceptive jerks,—these two positively were in London; and they thought so little of it, that their minds were gone. They would not say a word, to hurt the feelings of Aunt Snacks, who set this down to their abashment; but as soon as she was gone, they declared in one breath, that Exeter was much the finer city; and that London was all trees, and little windows, and big spikes, without any Fore-street, for the folk to come together.

And the more they saw of our vast metropolis, the less they thought of it, and the more they wanted to be back again, in a town where they knew the people. There was nobody, in this stuck-up place, even to touch his hat to them; and although they never looked for it around their house at home, they liked to have it done, and contrived to let their tradesman know, if his young men failed to do it. They felt that they were downright strangers here, and could not expect to be saluted, and must get accustomed to be passed, like posts. They saw that it was reasonable; but they did not like it.

To the acclimatized urban mind (degenerating into the less urbane), few things are more wondrous, than the memories of their " country cousins."　If a genuine Yorkshire, or Devonshire man—before the railways spoiled them both—ever espied, in a country lane, a Londoner trying to enjoy himself, and met him again, after changeful years, as a cock upon his own— or rather let us say, as a gentleman treading his own street, the rustic would hail him, and invite him to a parley, and tell him what his hat and waistcoat were, when faded from the owner's memory.　That gentleman's large heart might be fervent with great business; but the other would never let him go, until he declared that he remembered all about it.

When Mrs. Giblets, and her daughter Mary, walking in a broad North-western street, suddenly espied the red-faced man, they did not by any means act thus; but endeavoured to preserve their dignity.　They gave one another a nudge, to point perception, and enjoin discretion; and then they walked past him, with their bonnets turned aside, and their countenances lost in many ribands of eclipse.　Mr. Gaston caught a glimpse of bright country colour, and marched on, none the wiser. But they, with a spirit beyond their wont, and inspired perhaps by the air of town, turned, and at sagacious distance followed, to see what became of that very odious man. To find out where he lived, would be a precious feather in their caps; for Mr. Tucker had reproached himself, over and over again, for letting that visitor go, without knowing more about him.

"Mary, you leave it all to me. But your eyes are more younger like." Mrs. Giblets spoke with some excitement, because she was obliged to walk rather fast, and she had just been enjoying a long look at a turtle, as the relict of a mayor was bound to do, and she had longed to go in, and tell them who she was; and afterwards it made her sigh to walk, not for two thoughts of the animal, but only from remembering what her husband said, when the silver cradle was sent home, with a lace coverlet, and a Bristol turtle in it; for if any one knew how to do things well, the Barnstaple people in those days did. "Mary, you push on afront; he wouldn't know you again, so soon as me; because you be scarcely come to any size yet; and his cousin, Sir Courtenay, had acquaintance of your father, unless he were a story-teller, which I do believe of him. Keep you on, my dear, because you are so limber; and you may surely count on me behind—the same as they put the pelisses here—to come a long way afterwards. But be sure that you walk fittily."

Mary, like a child, was proud as Punch, to be so important, and to walk alone in the perilous streets of London; however, she preserved discretion, and walked fittily, even when her dear mamma was a hundred yards behind her. For the red-faced man strode along at good speed; and short Devonshire legs had to go two for one, to keep him anywise in view.

At length, in a place where the street narrowed into a road, without windows on either side, Mr. Gaston stopped, at a door in a high wall, unlocked it, and entered, and slammed the door behind him. A little further on, there were large folding gates, with real timber trees overhanging them; such an entrance to a mansion standing back in its own grounds, as Mary had seen in the outskirts of Exeter, but did not expect to find in London. "It must be some very great man that lives there, a nobleman at least, and perhaps a prince," Mary

Giblets said to her mother, when she met her coming round the corner with an anxious heart; "don't cough, mother, or he will hear you. I dare say he is inside the wall, now just. He looked back once, and I thought I should have dropped. It was just the way he looked at me, when I skipped through the stile of the little ham, where the bull was."

"Don't you be put upon your ropes, my dear," Mrs. Giblets answered calmly, though her clothes were hot; "if it is a prince as lives behind this wall, it never can be Red-face himself. He may be the butler, or the man-cook; for you heard what your Uncle Snacks said yesterday. They keep a man to roast and boil, in London, because of their complexions being cooler. And like enough, that is why he hath a ruddy countenance. But come you in here, and have a bun, dear heart. It is a little shop; and I love a little shop, because it looks like double-bakes. And if they don't know nothing else in London, they know better than hath visited our country, how to keep the glasses and the plates together."

These two ladies were not only thirsty, as ladies nearly always are, but also hungry to a very large extent. .For the air of London,

with its fine circulation, brings into the upper
stomach of the recent visitor a very delightful
(although to the slower mental faculties im-
perceptible) recognition of prime joints, revolving
at the bright well-springs of all that smoke.
Possibly, that is not the cause, or only one
among many; but the upshot is the same.
When people from the country come to London,
they are hungry at the end of every street, or
sometimes at the beginning.

"I don't know why I should ask, I am
sure," Mrs. Giblets said to the pastry-cook,
as he would have been called in Devonshire; "for we have such a number of large
houses in our parish; but do you happen to
know, sir, who lives across the road, inside
that wall? It looks so respectable, and rare
in London."

"I conclude, ma'am," answered the pastry-
cook, "you are only just come from the
country?"

"Well, sir, yes; to some extent. But we
know a great deal about London ways; and
every day makes a difference. We are accustomed to a city; and this does not seem to be
one."

"You are right, ma'am. We are quite in the

country here. Two and eightpence; fourpence change."

"But you should not speak with so much haste. Mary, my dear, look in my purse. I thought I put down three and sixpence. There was four and sixpence in that end. Oh no, I see; I beg your pardon, sir. But you have not told me, who lives in there."

"Well, ma'am, that is easier asked than answered; for they shut themselves up, like a convent almost, instead of doing any good to trade. But the house belongs to Lord Delapole; and, for all I know, he may be living in it."

"But surely you must know. You must feel some interest. I do not ask, out of mere curiosity. We happen to have some knowledge of a gentleman, who has just gone in, at the door up there. He paid us a visit, not so very long ago."

"Oh, you know Mr. Gaston, do you? A very nice gentleman, no doubt. Ladies, you had better go, and ask him about his own business; for he knows it best."

"How horribly rude these London people are!" Mrs. Giblets exclaimed, as they walked away. "They positively seem to care no more about you, the moment they have got your two and eightpence. However, we know the place now, Mary, dear; and we will set your Uncle Snacks to work. He must be the cleverest man in London, to have made such a fortune, in such a horrid place."

CHAPTER IX.

HEARTY KINDNESS.

IF ever anything has been proved to the satisfaction of mankind, it would seem to be their assimilation to the substance wherein they deal. A man who desires to improve his character, or confirm his principles (when he finds them beginning to be honest) must strictly withhold his steps from many paths of life, that should be straight, but only run straightway down-hill. Why are the greatest statesmen of the age far beyond credence of the most credulous? Because they have so long handled liars, that they follow their turns, and fall into them. Why is the most eminent British general inclined to quake, when returning thanks, on behalf of our noble army? Not because he ever felt fear himself; but from handling so many short-service soldiers, fugitive as a cheap French jelly.

On the other hand, to deal in good stiff stuff,

sets a man up, and puts core into him. A man who sells wire-netting, when requested to quote lowest prices, at wholesale rate, by post to-morrow (after a long interview, and a half inclination to come down), stiffens up again, and writes—" Dear sir; We are sorry to have quoted our price too low. Upon examination of our books we find"—something that rose in his conscience only. Whereas a good dealer in soft woollen nets can scarcely refuse any reasonable offer.

Throughout the years, which Mr. Caleb Tucker had spent in honest business, the timber chiefly in demand was oak. For every sort of work that was meant to last, in exposure to the wind and rain, people insisted upon having oak; and the blessings of free-trade (which, like those of Isaac, have descended upon the wrong head hitherto) had not yet filled our walls with cracks, and our diaphragms with quaking. This power of material had helped to consolidate Mr. Tucker's character, so that he could read the most important letters, without losing half a mouthful of his breakfast.

" Dear Uncle Caleb," said the one upon the table, " mother, and I want, oh so sadly, to be home again with you! There are no cob-walls here, and no flowers, unless you pay a lot of money for them; and a little cracked cabbage you would take to the pig-sty, costs twopence halfpenny, and impudence too. There are plenty of nice people, but they live so far apart, that you may go miles without seeing them; and even then, they have no time to spare."

"What a number of complaints—poor little Mary!" Uncle Caleb muttered, at the bottom of three pages; "well, it will teach them to enjoy their home. Halloa! What is this? I must read slowly."

"We have come across a thing, that you ought to know; and I am afraid that I cannot tell it clearly. Do you remember that gentleman, who came on horseback, in the spring, and behaved so badly? You were quite upset by his bad manners, because you would not answer all his crooked questions. You doubted very much, whether he had given his right name; and you talked about going to the gentleman on Dartmoor; but old Jerry fell so lame, that you could not do it; and you said that you did not like to write about it. It seems that his name was right enough, and better than his nature, as we say. We met him on the streets, about a week ago, and found out where he lives, and all about him. He seems to be a steward, or agent, or whatever it is, to a wealthy nobleman, who has a great house, all walled in, almost like a country place. And he is a very strange man, they say, and may go off at any time. Uncle Snacks knows a great deal about him, because of his being in the railway line; and this lord will not let them come through a field of his, without fighting for it. He seems to have no one to care about him, except the servants, and it makes him fret; for he lost his grandson a little while ago, a fine boy, but he caught the small-pox. And not so very long ago, he had lost his son, the father of his grandson; and they say that he has another son somewhere, who disgraced himself shockingly, back in the war-time, and never could get on with his father. But now Mr. Gaston tends the whole of his concerns, they say, and he is accounted unusual honest; although they live like cats and dogs, for his lordship has a temper, and so has Mr. G. Uncle Snacks told me to write all this; and mother says no lawyer could have done it better."

"Neither he could," said Mr. Tucker, going to the fire, for some more hot fried potatoes; "though it requireth to be read again, to know which is which, of all them, 'he's.' 'Tis late in life for me to meddle with the concerns of other folk however. But here comes different sign manual to the foot of it. Must have my thick specks, they new ones is like shop-fronts."

With the help of his thick horn spectacles, which he was not allowed to wear on Sundays —and this was a Sunday, as his breakfast proved, for he had sausages with his fried potatoes—the dealer in oak, of former days, made out the thin scrawl of the jobber in shares, whose hand he had never seen before.

"Dear sir. If convenient, you should come up. Mary says, that you know all about things going on, I won't say where. Robbery, which might be regretted when too late, and worse things to come afterwards. With best respects, yours faithfully, John Snacks."

"Well! I did intend to go to church. And I will go to church, because I hear the bells," Mr. Tucker thought slowly, and with memories of childhood; "the best ideas always come in church, because they have no business."

He did as he had said, and came to this conclusion, that his duty by no means required him to go to London, upon other people's business; but that it might be a matter to repent of, if neglected altogether. Old Jerry (the only horse he owned at present), although getting better, was scarcely fit to climb stony places with a tender feeling; and his master, after looking at him in the afternoon, resolved to take the chariot of Pug-ley, towards the heights of Christowell. Pugsley had no right to carry passengers for hire, and no one must go over Exe-bridge with him, unless it were a child of tender years, such as Rose Arthur used to be. But if Master Timothy discovered on the road a respectable wayfarer, looking weary, his manner was to ask him whether he would ride, in a social rather than commercial spirit; though it tended, by-and-by perhaps, towards half-a-crown.

The carrier, and the timber merchant, knew one another on the road of old, and cherished mutual respect. And Mr. Arthur, from time to time, had sent a present of fruit, or flowers, or honey, to his city friend, by good care of Pugsley. Therefore, after long discourse, and easy turns of summer lanes, Mr. Tucker was set down within a mile of Lark's Cot, in the early afternoon. Timothy would have gone further with him; but the old gentleman's legs were good, and as there was nothing in the cart for the captain, he would not work the old horse on. How to get home, was another question; but he was sure of hospitality.

"Why what a lovely place it is!" Mr. Tucker could not help exclaiming, as he crossed the little meadow, and descried the cottage, nestled in with fruitful trees, and plumed with roses, and honeysuckles; "it was not like this, when I bought it for him, but looked all bleak and shivering. All the work of his own hands. Ah, that is the way to fence the world out. I wonder if they will let me in. Pugsley told me, to pull this wire."

He pulled the wire, and a bell, that hung outside the porch, made answer; and presently Moggy, the maid, came out, with an apron over her head, because she had curled her hair on Sunday; and after a parley in broad dialect, she went to look for her master, up the stream. In a very short time, Mr. Tucker was resting in the pleasant bower by the brook, while the captain was opening a bottle of cider, and Rose was gone to the house, to speed the prospects of an early dinner.

"I am heartily glad to see you once more, in the place that owes everything to you," Mr. Arthur said, as he filled a long bright glass, with brighter liquid. "You see, that I am quite a native now, and trying to advance upon the native ways. Tell me what you think of that. A perfect cure for gout, and rheumatism. How many kinds of apples are there in it?"

"Well, perhaps twenty; or there might be fifty," Mr. Tucker replied, with the fresh colour flowing into his cheeks, and a polish on his lips; "it is fine enough for fifty, as we say."

"Three, and no more," said the captain slowly, and with stress upon every word; "three, and no more, is the secret, or at least the main secret, of the way to do it. But who knows an apple from a pippin here, or a pippin from a crab, or a crab from a service? You may talk for ever; but they only know, that ' their veythers always did this, or thiccy; and they don't need to be no wiser than their veythers was.' They admit that mine is better; they can't help doing that; and if any one is ill, they send for it. But as for budging out of their own ways, or trying to learn one tree from another—they tell me, they actually have told me several times, that it goes against Genesis, and the Parables!"

"Perhaps it is all the better for them,"—Mr.

Tucker was a Tory of good type,—"to be contented with their ancient ways. They make it anyhow, and they drink it anyhow, and they thrive upon it soberly. But if their liquor was like this, they would soon be above their work, and be getting gout, for the sake of such a medicine. People are always gabbling now, about elevating everybody. Nobody knows what it means; and I would rather see them hanged; because there you are. Good health to you, my lord—for so I believe you are by this time."

"I have not received any notice of it; and hope that you may be mistaken, Mr. Tucker. It would be the worst thing, that could befall me. In the outer world at least."

"We never know, what is good for us;" it appeared to the timber-merchant, that it must be good to be a lord; "and I am too old to be carried away, by any ups and downs of life. But at first sight, sir, it looks like promotion; and I promised myself some pleasure, in offering first congratulations. But excuse my saying that you take peculiar views of things."

"No, Mr. Tucker, I do not. I look at things, as every gentleman, and every man of honesty, in whatever station, must look at them. You know part of my story, but not all. When you know the whole, you will merely say, that in my place, you must have done the same. But tell me, what have you heard about me, or rather about my relatives?"

"It appears from this letter," the old man answered, spreading his niece's long epistle on his knee, and feeling (as a true Briton must) some pride in this, connection with the peerage, "that your elder brother is dead, my lord; I have not the exact date of his death; but his departure from this world seems certain."

"I have heard of that. I avoid newspapers; as I have good cause to do. However, that came to my knowledge, through an accident. But before you go further, let me beg of you one thing, in which I am sure you will oblige me. Do not call me 'my lord;' but speak to me, just as you always used to do."

Mr. Tucker bowed, and smiled, and then proceeded. "Well, sir, I peruse the papers; as a man in my humble position must do. But I was not aware, until I got this letter, that your brother's only child was dead. He appears to have been carried off by small-pox. Sad indeed for any one, but most sad for the heir to an Earldom, and large property, where the railways want to come."

"I am grieved to hear it, for my father's sake, as well as the poor little boy's. Are you certain, that it is so?"

"If you will kindly take this, and read it, you will know as much as I know. The women may pick up things amiss. But brother Snacks must be an accurate man, to have made all his money; and he backs it up."

Mr. Arthur took the letter, and read the part of Mary's writing that concerned himself, and the brief lines of the new-found uncle, of whom Uncle Caleb felt dire jealousy already.

"Every word of it looks like the truth," said Mr. Tucker; "though you never can tell nowadays. Mary is a truthful maid, as can be; but that sort gets imposed upon. And what do you say to it now, if you please?"

"There may be a little exaggeration," the captain answered quietly; "there always is that, in a case of this kind. But most of it is true. Who is that Mr. Gaston? He paid you a visit, last spring, I see."

"Yes, and a fine sort of a visit. I should live behind a river, if such visitors were common. We did the best we could for him, in our unpretentious way; and I offered him refreshment, to the best of my ability; but he showed himself unworthy, and made light of my intentions, because I would not furnish him with all information about you. I ought to have written to you about it; but I thought it would be better, to come and see you; but somehow or other, the time went by; and I humbly ask your pardon for neglect."

"Not at all. It is most kind of you to come now. You knew quite well, that I would not see the man; and to hear of him, would only have annoyed me. But what in the world could he have wanted of me? Did he give you any idea?"

"I don't think that he wanted to see you, but to know for his own purposes, where to find you. Possibly to prevent other people from seeing you. But I will tell you what he said, that you may judge for yourself; after making all allowance for his off-hand style, and remembering that he would try, most likely, to deceive me."

Mr. Tucker took a pinch of snuff, to stimulate his memory, and then told his host, as correctly as need be, the purport of George Gaston's words about him.

"Did you hear what became of him, when he left you?" Mr. Arthur asked, after listening to this tale; "or whether he went on with his inquiries about me? Having contrived to find you out, he would be pretty sure to find me too."

"That is not so certain; for you live in a place so secluded; and he would not know your name. But I saw no more of him, and heard no more of him, until I got this letter. Only I have a suspicion, that he went to a firm of low land-jobbers, in the suburbs of St. Thomas. I met one of them in the timber-yard soon after— for I go there, now and then occasionally—and he called out to me, like a low fellow as he is— 'I say, old gentleman, can you give us a glass of rum?' Of course that proves nothing; but it struck me, at the moment, as a remarkable coincidence."

"You may depend upon it, you were right. He knew that I had bought land, through your good offices, and he seems to have known my purpose too. From such people, who know you, and keep no doubt a jealous eye upon your doings, he would speedily discover, for a small fee, all they knew; and then put them to find out what they did not know. I must act upon the presumption, that this man knows me, my name, my dwelling-place, and all about me.

By the way, a thought strikes me—but I will find that out to-morrow. Now what can the motives of this Gaston be? A revengeful, malicious-looking man, you say? But I cannot have wronged him. His name is quite unknown to me."

"Well, sir, he must have some motive; and you may be pretty sure, that it is a bad one. Perhaps to get your property for himself, and blacken you to the poor old nobleman."

"I do not see how it can be that. The property is in strict settlement. If all that you have heard is true, after my father's time, I must take it, if I choose to do so; except the merely personal part, which is trifling, or at any rate, used to be so. I cannot see what this man can mean, by hunting me out, and then leaving me in the dark."

"Never mind, sir, you may be quite clear, that he means wrong, and you must take him for an enemy, a bitter, and crafty enemy. If he had meant to do the honest thing, he would have found you out by public means; or if there was anything against that, he would have come to you like a man, as soon as he discovered you."

"No doubt he would; if indeed he has discovered me; and of that there cannot be much question." The captain looked around, as if he would like to know the opinion of his trees, at this cruel disturbance of their master, and to ask them whether they would break their hearts, at the loss of the man who loved them so. The trees however showed no concern.

"I am sure I cannot tell, sir," the timber-merchant said, while the other was reflecting sadly; "you know best, what suits your life; but if I may say so, without being rude, within the four seas there may be four men, and no more, that would be sorry to be found out so—to be called to great wealth, and a high position, and with a dear child to inherit it. Miss Rose has grown into the loveliest young lady; and her manners are as lovely as herself. For one thing, you may thank the Lord, sir—if I am not to call you, by your proper title—and that is the opportunity you have had, of bringing up a sweet simple nature, without any of the spoil-ings of the world. She never would have been like what she is, if her lines had fallen among gay rich people."

"There is much truth in what you say, my friend. And you may be sure that it has occurred to me; though nothing in the world could have spoiled my Rose. But it is on her account, that I am most perplexed. If it were not for that darling child, I could act according to my own wishes, which are very simple, and have long been shaped. But her interests must be thought of, more than my desires."

"Certainly they ought to be. No just man could think twice, upon such a point as that." Mr. Tucker spoke decisively, and almost sternly; for he was a man of strong clear sense, and had often condemned, in his own shrewd mind, what he thought to be the sensitive weakness of the other. "You may have your own ideas," he continued, "and your own views of happiness, and contentment; upon which I have never ventured to intrude, in spite of your flattering confidence in me. For yourself, you have a perfect right to judge; but for others—however it is not my place—— "

"No, it is not your place," Mr. Arthur answered, looking at the old man gratefully, "to offer advice, without a thorough knowledge of all that has happened to us. This you have never had, for various reasons; most of which are now gone by. You knew very little of my affairs; and yet, through some sympathy, you took my part."

" Ay, that I did ; and I couldn't tell the reason, unless it was the trouble on the both of us. Your dear wife was dead ; and mine was gone ; and a faithful partner she had been. ' Caleb,' she used to say, ' never you be hard ; it comes so easy to be hard ; no fear of nobody neglecting that. But it needeth a man, to be soft, my dear.' Perhaps her meaned, that the women wasn't so. But goodness knows, she never meant no harm. There I be talking, as if I wasn't eddicated! All of us does, when we thinks of trouble ; from the way we go on, in the natural times. And then you came, with your hat-band on ; and there was no complaint outside your eyes. And I was dwelling upon her, that moment."

The turn of the old man's mind had brought the long review of his own life up ; and the captain, having much of his own to look back on, waited for his sigh, before speaking again. For the sigh of the old, is the spirit's adieu to a mournful subject, until next time.

" But we must have another talk about this cider," Mr. Tucker continued, to save abruptness ; " it should be indeed a thing to talk of, if a stranger could beat all Devonshire, like this ! When you have time, sir, whenever you have time, I shall be happy to meet you, on that subject; for I used to fancy that I understood it, and I made an improvement in the presses once; and I ought to have had a patent for it."

"I hope to have many good talks about it; and especially about the best fruit for it," the captain answered briskly; "for the Devonshire apples puzzle me; partly by their local names, and their infinite variety, but still more, by their general badness. I can go on talking about fruit, for ever, when I find any one to care about the subject, which I scarcely ever do. I suppose, we are all born with a turn for something; however the turn of our lives may obscure it. But I see, by the top of the kitchen chimney, that our plain dinner is as ripe as a good fig. My daughter will call us, in about two minutes. You have walked far to-day, and you ought to be hungry; or at any rate, you must be tired, my good friend."

"Not as I knows of," Mr. Tucker answered; for Devonsire legs go up and down, by power of habit, without much strain. "But at my time of life, that comes afterwards, to think of."

"You shall not walk another step, to-night; except to my cottage, and a stroll by-and-by, if you fancy it, in my garden. We will make you as comfortable, as we can ; and my Rosie is no bad hand at that. You have been a very true friend to us, Mr. Tucker. I never like to press my affairs upon any one ; for we all make a great deal too much fuss, about ourselves. But if you would like to hear my little story, to which you have never had the key as yet, you would do me a favour by listening by-and-by ; and even a greater one, by your advice upon it."

"Sir, I may say, though I am not curious, that I have very often longed to know it."

"Here comes my darling! She shall go to bed early. For I would not disturb her, on any account. And then, if you are not too tired, you shall know, what has driven me to this peculiar life ; though I do not complain of it, and wish for nothing better. The happiest of mankind is he, who does what he likes, and yet works hard."

CHAPTER X.

JACK O' LANTERN.

JOHN SAGE had now spent several weeks in Colonel Westcombe's service, giving, and receiving the most lofty satisfaction. Without the warmest urgency, on the part of the pisci-capturists (for a fish is not to be called a fish now, and everything connected with him is pisci-something), the colonel never would have spared this wisest, and therefore best, member of the human race. But it had been felt on every side, that John was the only one who could do it; and even at Touchwood Park, it was whispered, that old Sage was the first to put it into Master Dicky's head. But John, with a guinea in the lining of his waistcoat, took a view of all of them; and walked away in silence. For, if so be, he had boasted much, he could have done no less than stand treat.

He was perfectly capable now of standing

treat, and might have had credit for a side of
bacon, at Betty Cork's shop in Christowell.
But he shunned all extravagance, took his pint
as usual, in exchange for good advice, and
enjoyed his three-halfpenny rasher with his
wife, when he came home on Sundays, to
applaud Parson Short. And when he rode
down the hill, from Dartymore desert, on the
colonel's old gray pony, there might have been
found in front of him, by insidious search
beneath his old hill-coat, a bag of some capacity,
not idly so endowed, but exerted to its utmost,
to contain good things. For he had advised
the colonel's cook, how to fetch her sweetheart
round, when hankering after less peppery
charms; and the female heart excels the male,
in being grateful *gratis*. And, though the high
principles of old John were far too prudent to
accept the very sweetest essence of unlawful
meat, and compelled him indeed to keep a
sharp look-out, that nobody else did such a
thing, he found himself enabled, with all
imaginable honesty, to secure some peaceful
tributes to domestic virtue. The colonel knew,
that he went forth in marching order, on a
Saturday, victualled for his camp that night,
among the Pixies, and the Kists; which de-

manded body, and spirit too, in the liquid half of nourishment. And the only reason old John had, for putting his coat upon his bag, as he rode into Christowell, and buying, in a public manner, that rasher for three-halfpence, was that if he failed to do so, the hospitable feeling of his neighbours would compel his wife to give a tea-party, as soon as ever his back was turned.

If ever a man deserved such things, and better than the best of them, John Sage used to feel that man, inside his own shirt, as he rode proudly down the hill. Full of the spirit of the moor (which always rushed upon him gloriously, as soon as he was off it), he despised these people, who had lain down here, like a pack of cowards, asleep all night, and were coming out now, in their shirt-sleeves, after being lathered by their wives—for the barber could not find soap for any one, under a penny —to be shaved; and then (as if they had done a brave thing) would go back, and blow the bellows, till the kettle boiled. And all of these, when they looked at John, considering where he had passed the night, instead of being critical of what he had in front of him, were almost afraid to say, " Marnin' to 'e, Maister ! "

In such a lofty character, there scarcely should have been a single vestige of conceit. And knowing what he was, he strove his utmost, not to let other people know. But, with the usual wilfulness of fame, the less he spoke, the more she blew his trumpet; until he could scarcely have his pipe in peace, and was obliged to bar the door, before he filled it. And then he used to meditate upon his many dangers, and flourish his stick in self-defence, until he broke his pipe-stem. For Weist-Tor, where he had to pass the night of almost every Saturday, was enough to make a man enjoy existence, when he got away from it.

"Sage, I shall be glad to have a talk with you, this evening," Mr. Short said, when he came out of church, one fine Sunday in August, with the congregation drawn up outside, for the secular postscript to his good Church-words; "come up about seven o'clock, if you can." This vicar, after learned and impartial research, had come to the definite conclusion, that Sunday ended at six p.m.

John Sage thought it hard, to go all that way, with his legs still bowed from so much saddle, and his supper, by that time, sure to be inside him. But his mind was up with admiration; for the sermon had not contradicted his opinions; and he saw that the parson meant no less than half-a-crown. So he promised to go; and in good time went, recalling to his mind that he never could have won his fine rise of wages, without the parson's word. Moreover, he valued Mrs. Aggett highly; and he knew that excessive self-respect was the only power that could have stopped her, from coming on a Sunday afternoon, to gather sweet particulars about the cook at Westcombe. Therefore he opened the vicarage gate, with a mind at once loyal, and lofty.

"How famously you look, John!" Mr. Short observed, as soon as the wisdom of the village was shown in; "you have recovered all the substance of your wrestling days. You used to be a fine hand at it, I am told, with a trick of the inner crook, of your own invention."

"Ay, sir, I have drowed a good few vormerly. But there bain't no wrastlin' fit to speak of now. Last time I went to see 'un, I were compelled for to up sticks."

"I can understand the wrath of a scientific hand. They tell me it is come to a mere bout of kicking. But you were the champion, at one time, Sage."

"No, sir, no. I wor not big enow for that.
I could drow any man, within two stun of me.
But there used to be men, as could take me up
with one hand, and shake me like a handker-
cher. What use of playing, with such men as
them? But their mothers never bring forth
such men now."

"I am afraid that is true," said Mr. Short,
considering himself with sadness; "I fear that
the Englishmen get smaller, like onions sown
where they grew last year. But, John, let us
come down from such great subjects. You are
doing very nicely, over there, at Colonel Westcombe's?"

"Well, sir, I never complain. Vact is, I be
too old, to begin complaining."

"Did you ever leave off, John?" the parson
asked, with a quick look, such as he gave them
in church, when he hit their thoughts, with
his own almost. They always liked this, because it showed that they were men; and now
old John grinned—which he very seldom did,
else would his fame have been far smaller.

" A' maight be better; and a' maight be wuss."

"That means, that it is as good as can be.
And you know as well as I do, John, that you
never had such a kind master before. Now,

if you take advantage of him, if you sit upon a stump, and go to sleep, if you get too much into his back kitchen, or put too much into your bag on a Saturday night——"

"However did they rob you, Maister? You be that sharp, I should have thought it were not compuss!"

"If you do such things as I have said, John Sage, you will not only lose the best place you ever had, but you will be a disgrace to Christowell, and to me who recommended you. I know, that you are a very honest man; but I also know that very honest men begin to slide, under too much opportunity. Now when you come home, on a Sunday morning, bring your bag, like a man, without any coat over it."

"Passon, you be too bad; and a' most unlike a Christian, after all the holy things you be bound to think of, leastwise on the Sabbath day. I never wud a' drummed to you, a' church this morning, if I cud a' zeen the inside of your mind. I be dree score year and five of age, and no importation on my karákter yet. And who is there, as would come home across the moor, wi'out a bit of zummat, to the front of him?"

"Well, John, you know that I am speaking

for your good. You bear a high character, and you deserve it. Whatever is given to you, is your own ; if the proper people give it. But bring it as your own, without concealment. That was the first thing, I had to say to you. But I also have another thing, upon my own account. How often are you sent to pass the night, at Weist-Tor ? "

" Sometimes once a week, sometimes twice. According to the weather, and the doings of the birds. But I wudn't baide alone there, for a thousand pounds a'most. Joe cometh with me, always."

" Yes, I know. Your son Bill's boy. Colonel Westcombe employs him ; and it all helps up. You must have passed a dozen nights there, by this time. Have you ever seen anything particular ? "

" Sartin, sir. His Honour had a door put up, to keep the wind out ; and us always goes together, to look out ; afore bedding down upon the hathe. No, I never draw my money wi'out arning of it. Sometimes 'twould be the moon, and another time the stars, or leastwise the clouds in front of 'un. And once 'twas Jack o' lantern, so sure as I be living ! "

" Ah ! " said Mr. Short, " that does seem odd.

I have heard of him a hundred times, but never seen him. I would ride fifty miles, to see that thing. You shall have a guinea, John, if you can put me up to it. I shall come, and visit you, some night, when it is likely. But what did Jack o' lantern do, that night you saw him? And did you go down, to look after him?"

"The Lord forbid! Why, passon, you know, as well as I do, 'tis sartin death to volly 'un. No, no, us barred the door, and kept each other company. Joe be as brave a'most, as I be."

"How long is it, since you saw that sight, or peeped at it, and ran away, you brave generation?"

"Well, sir, maight a' been a fortnight mainly. I don't keep no account of time, too partiklar. The Lord hath ordained for us martels not to do so, with our eyes looking forward to the kingdom. But it wur of a Tuesday; that I be sure of, by reason of the time to kill the fowls."

"Tuesday is the day, that a sheep is always killed. How many Tuesdays, have you been there? Try to recollect; you are famous for your memory."

"Never of a Tuesday, but that once. Nobody can put up they fowls but me, wi'out a clack coming out o' their tongues. They be such a noisy set, to that side o' the moor. And once the good lady, that, keepeth to her chimber, heer'd them a gruntin', when it wur done badly; and his honour come out, and I told him they were vules, and cudn't administer kingdom come, to a young cock with dacency; and so he saith, 'You do it then; John, you do it for the future time.' And I did sixteen on 'em, wi'out a murmur; and ever since then, I has to do it. But happened one Tuesday, they was to have a holiday; and that wur the night, us seed Jack o' lantern."

"Very well, Sage. Now will you manage to do them early, Tuesday next, unless they are to have another holiday? And then, to be up on the hill, that night; and I will come to you, to see Jack o' lantern. If we see him, you shall have a guinea; and if we don't, you shall have a crown. Don't say a word of it, to any one; unless your master gives you orders not to go. If he does that, just say, that it is my particular wish that you should be there; and then, he will be sure to let you come. But I don't want young Master John to know a word about it. If he did he would insist on coming too."

"Sartin sure, he wud. He be a push-about

young gentleman. No, no, I wun't let 'un hear tell of it. Passon Short, it shall be done, ezakly to your bidding."

Any man, who has not been on Weist-Tor at night, or at any rate towards evening, might underrate the courage of John Sage, and his grandson Joe, in sleeping there. It is perfectly true, that they barred the door, and stopped their ears, if they heard a noise, which it was wiser to ignore than to inquire of; but still every right-minded person knows, that if love laughs at locksmiths, a power (too often supreme in love) ridicules the blacksmith too. Can any bolt, or bar, keep out the Devil?

There is not only this to be considered, but also the general tone of the place, without such visitations. At any time of day, this is very bad indeed, because there is nothing to enrich, or even soften it. Somewhat as a man of rugged nature, or a roguish elephant, hardens into his own bad seams, from lack of female society. But when the night comes down from heaven, or deepens, without any sign of heaven, up the long hollows, and over the grey waste, fantastic things stand forth of shadow, and images of fear perplex the distance.

"Bravo! Here you are! Well done, my

friends," Mr. Short exclaimed, for he was glad to see them, as the long day went to rest; "what a large place it is! I began to think, that I should never find you."

"Good eyes be needed, to find the biggest man, as ever trod the earth, or the biggest thing, he hath ever piled upon it, in the loose ways the land hath here about. Little Joe, and me, be like a pair of murmets, hurning about on a big tombstone. Passon, here be pulpits, and the word of God to preach from." John Sage put down the bone of ham, that he was sucking, upon a kistvaen, and gazed largely around.

"I have been here before," answered Mr. Short, who never would be capped with his own hat; "but one forgets this sort of place. Did you bring a bone for me, John?"

"Must needs be a dry one, to agray with such as you, sir. But coom inzaide the little 'ouze, sir. A' be done winderful, winderful golaightly."

"So it is. Very clever, very cumpuss, as you say; and with nicks in the rock, for you to hide in, if the enemy beat down the bar. And here you sleep, on this sweet heather, as plum as any horse-hair. It might blow, and rain, for fifty hours, without a drop, or a breath upon you. You have chosen your place well, with

the scoop of the crag to shelter you, and the
standing slabs for your side-posts, and your
little roof of furze, and ling, the colour of the
rocks around. The pixies themselves could
scarcely find you, unless you make a fire here.
But, where do you keep the pony, John?"

"Well, sir, he never wandereth far, unless
the moor-ponies comes a 'ticin of 'un. But he
hath a bed of 's own close by, under the big
loggin stone. Us can hear him gruntin', as he
drameth; and a' maketh rare company, by night.
But, passon, 'tis an unkid place, and requaireth
a brave man, with the fear of the Lord around
him, for to smoothe his eyes to slape."

"You have had your supper, and you want
your sleep," replied Mr. Short; for he never
encouraged what he called " Psalmodic piety;"
and he knew that all men, who live under the
sun, must follow him with their inclinations;
"take little Joe inside, and bar the door. I
shall want no help from you. But show me
first, where the Jack o' lantern was."

Old Sage saw, that his courage was not held
in very high esteem; but he felt, within himself, that it lacked no vindication. Therefore, he was satisfied with showing, by some
general signs, where the dancing light had

shone; and then, to keep all blame away, he called his grandson to hear him say—"The Lord have mercy upon thee, passon! Thou bee'st a minister of He. If thy horders draiveth thee, to vollow up the Evil One, us will come, and zee, when thou hast catched un." With these liberal sentiments, he pulled his head in, and barred the door.

Mr. Short had inherited much, from his grandfather, the admiral, of even greater value than the Victory chronometer. Among the best of these things, were sturdy courage, and strong love of justice; both of which seem to be evaporating now, into clouds of magnanimity. The parson sat down, in a square niche of rock, which fitted him better than if made to measure; and from the pockets of his shooting-coat, which was made of stout dark fustian, he drew forth some little things he had prepared, with a hope that they might prove useful. There was no kind of fire-arm among them; nor even what was then called a "life-preserver;" but there was a running noose, of supple round leather, and some strong silk rope from his own window-curtains, and a steel-chain, ending with a short spring-loop. He considered these a little, and arranged them, so that he could pull out any

one, or all, when needed; and then, making
up his mind for some hours of patience, lit his
pipe, and calmly watched the deepening of the
darkness.

Not even a sheep, or a dump of a pony, broke
the contracting gloom before him, with a spot
of movement.   Down the hillside, slabs of
granite. tilted against one another, or leaning
out of the earth, or piled (like tombstones, in
pictures of the Resurrection) glanced the faint
descent of light, still overlapping the western
crest; upon which the cumbrous tor was losing
its jagged blackness, in the growth of night.
The restless wind, (that ruffles the scanty herb-
age there by daytime, and bares the edges of
desolation,) after a few weak, moaning shivers,
sank into the universal calm; and there was not
even the twinkle of a star, to mar the dark
brown depth of night.   " If ever he wanted his
lantern, he will want it now," thought Mr.
~~Sharp~~; "but how deadly cold the air is
getting !"

He arose, and flapped his strong round breast,
with thickset arms, and solid hands; and then
walked to and fro, for half an hour, on a narrow
track of safety. at the bottom of the tor.   Below
this, yawned a great rock circle, of the kind that

is called "Druidical," though probably quite as true a work of nature, as a fairy ring is. To rush through this, in the darkness, would be to tempt at least a broken leg; and he had marked his track, to the right or left, before the gloom became so deep. Also he had brought a strong oak staff, to feel his way down the hill, and to assure it; for his chief fear was of bogs. But these are either slightly luminous, or else intensely black, upon a summer night like this. Whatever he did, he must preserve his presence of mind, and walk with care.

At last, when he was almost beginning to weary of the shivering solitude, a faint light twinkled far away; and then disappeared, and then shone clearer, down the valley towards the right. Then, it began to rise and fall, and stop sometimes, and even vanish, as something intercepted it; but upon the whole, it was coming nearer; like the light of a vessel beating up towards the bar. Although the weather, and the time of year, were suitable for that phosphoric proceeding, known as "Will o' the Wisp," in the north, and "Jack o' lantern," in the south of England, the parson, without thinking twice, was sure, that he had no pale spectre of that sort, before him. In that particular seam of

hill, up which the light was advancing, **there**
was no morass, nor even peaty quagmire; but **a**
little rill, running down a narrow bed of rock-
scoop, scarcely so wide as a mangle, and **tufts**
of gorse, interlaid with short sweet grass—
shelter, meat, and drink, and music, for **the**
serious-minded sheep. "Ah, he knows what
good mutton is; and perhaps that is why **he**
did not eat mine. Mother Aggett will so over-
flour it."

With these reflections, ill-suited perhaps **to**
the gravity of the moment, the vicar of Christowell made some steps, towards a clearer knowledge of the case before him. He knew, that he
was going to a perilous encounter, with a man
as superior to himself in size, as inferior alas, **in**
principle. But he relied upon the justice of his
cause—as everybody does, who ever goes **to**
war; and although his grandfather's clock was
gone, he had serious hopes of getting back some
rusty remnant of his other household gods.
But, just as he was setting forth, a squeaky little
voice came after him, and a little figure followed
it. "Oh, do 'e let me coom, passon; do 'e let
me coom, 'long of 'e."

"I am surprised to see you here, when all
good boys are fast asleep. Go back, Joe Sage,

to your grandfather." Mr. Short spoke crossly; for he warmly "undesired"—as the western improvers of our language put it—to have his little expedition talked of, all over Christowell, to-morrow. "Go you to bed," he said; "and tuck your little toes up."

"Grandfather be aveared of pixies, sir," said the boy, still holding on to him; "but I been to schule, outside of your parish; and I ain't got no faith, in none on 'em."

"Then, go back, you unhappy little sceptic," Mr. Short answered, without applause; for he knew what comes of that warty state of mind, which crop-up lads get into. "The birch is the right thing, for you to believe in."

Little Joe Sage was discouraged by this view of his intellectual advancement; and he went back slowly, till his footsteps dropped into the silence of the hill. But then he turned, and listened, and pursued the vicar, at safe distance, and with frequent palpitations of his small, but not ignoble heart.

Feeling his way down the steep, with his stick, and watching the movements of that light, the wary parson kept on steadily, until he came to a furzy bottom, where a small brook tinkled through. Here were many little windings, such as water brings to pass, and juts of sudden turn, and even a breadth, or two, of flat land among the furze. It was much too dark to make out all that; but according to the general manner of the moor, there would be short sweet pasture here, and gentle slopes to lie down upon, and herbs that improve both the flavour, and texture, of a conscientious mutton.

The Dartmoor sheep is a thoughtful fellow, who knows what a greedy world it is, and therefore sleeps with one eye open. As Mr. Short came down this hollow, two or three woolly forms rushed by him, elder members of the flock, who had taken the alarm, and made off betimes. But, whether from selfishness, or no worse than sleepy lapse of duty, they failed to raise the warning "baa," that should have stirred up their relatives.

"That fellow can't be far off now; and of course he will conceal his light; my best plan will be to get behind this ridge, and watch what he is up to." With these reflections, Mr. Short slipped quietly into some broken ground, commanding a little strip of pasture, hedged with bushes, and granite slabs. Here were at least a score of sheep; and the air was thick with their oily smell. By the aid of a feeble glance of light, partly from a lifting cloud, and partly from the water, and white gravel on the brink of it, the watcher could make out their position, and could guess at their different attitudes. Some were already afoot, and listening, with short ears pricked, and long bald noses pointed up, to catch the air; some were half-rising, with their weight thrown forward, and hind feet scratching on the ground, for leverage; while others, of the fatter order, still lay grunting, well aware that something was being talked about, but convinced that it was nothing, but a pack of stuff.

Among these last, was a very worthy wether, an excellent animal in truly prime condition, with a speciality of mind, which had enabled him to fatten in the right style, and must add superior relish to his body. Confident in his own integrity, and fitness to survive all other sheep,—though a butcher might have taken it for fitness to be killed,—this sheep declined all participation in the low misgivings of the leaner lot. For fat, when laid on in the proper places, enlarges, enriches, and ennobles the mind; as every one acknowledges, who has grown fat. But this sheep had little time for more self-gratulation. For suddenly, a long dark form was upon him. He found himself grasped, by the back of the neck, and raising his head to remonstrate, lost all further knowledge of existence. There was nothing of him left, but wool, and mutton; and a long carving-knife was stuck into the grass, among the last marks of his pretty nibbling teeth. "Rare bit of stuff that parson's knife is! The only prize he ever got at Oxford, I'll be bound. And no doubt he stole that from the buttery."

Mr. Short, as he heard that most untrue description of his university career (which had been good), found it very difficult to hold his peace. But keenly apprehensive of the *suo sibi cultro*, he kept his head down, and laboured not to grind his teeth. For he knew, that if he did prevail against this Ajax, it must be by the tactics of Ulysses. There stood the slayer,—as the grand speech has it,—but there was not a symptom of remorse as yet, and to-morrow's sun might announce, to Mrs. Aggett, the decease of the wrong man, the one who paid regularly eightpence halfpenny a pound, for all his mutton. "I will stick here, instead of being stuck;" thought Mr. Short, with that brevity which made his sermons so delightful.

The skilful slayer took his time as well. He

had once been famed for hospitality; and the
desertion of his friends, which ensued upon his
trouble, though it might have blunted, had not
wholly soured a nature capable of good. And
in fact, he was making preparations now for a
dinner-party, upon a good scale, to a highly
select list of rogues at the *Raven*. One, or
two of these had expressed some doubt, concerning the quality of Dartmoor mutton; because
they had only had it, as supplied by contract, at
the charges of the British prison-ratepayer. And
undoubted as their right was to good things, in
gaol (when restricted of their right to steal
them), not one of them had sat down to a good
juicy leg, till they came to believe, that there
was no such thing. This was enough to make
any man labour, when he had nothing else to
do, to establish his opinion, by some very careful work. Without this in view, Mr. Wenlow
perhaps would scarcely have come upon this
hunting-ground again, and at night; when a
sheep might be shot any day, or at any time
of night, with comfort. But it was his business
to regard things now; and whatever faults
there might be in his constitution, it was good
of him, thus to desire to impart the results of
his long experience in mutton. However, this

virtuous weakness led, as it too often does, to calamity.

It was a time of year, when meat must not be thumped about, or used as a weight to be "putted," or a hammer to make holes in its dear brother joints; as railway porters treat it now. Mr. Wenlow, understanding this, proceeded with hospitable care, to sling his good animal upon his back; so that the prime parts might ride well. With the aid of his lantern, which had been left in brief eclipse, he nicely corded the cold hind-feet together, then carefully wiped his knife, and thrust it into a sheath at his left side. Then, after blowing out his candle, and concealing it; with a trifle of a groan, he shouldered this fine weight of mutton, and found that he could manage it. Not that he meant to go, all the way home with it—for strong as he was, that would have tried him— but only to get to a cool dry place, where his prize might be stored, for future operations. "I ought to have him now," thought Mr. Short; "I will let him get tired; and then tackle him."

The sheepslayer, under his burden, walked with a long heavy stride, which prevented him from hearing any light sound of pursuit. So that, although the night was very dark, and still, the parson could keep him pretty well in view, with the help of the white body, hanging on his back. And it was not likely that a man, with such a load, would depart from the downward track, if he could help it. For the ground was uneven, though not bouldery, nor morassy; and a strong man had as much as he could do, to get along, with a weight, like a bag of potatoes, to stoop to, and small opportunity of picking every step. And sure enough, before very long, this began to come hard upon the wind of Mr. Wenlow. Mr. Short heard him begin to pant a little; and then he could see, that the sheep, upon his back, was swagging about, as if its death had been a dream, and it were trying to get up, to graze again.

"Now I will have him, as he had Mother Aggett, and cord him fast to his own dinner."

Meditating thus, and with presence of mind in every quick joint of his body, the vicar of Christowell, who was a wonderful hand at knotty subjects, came swiftly behind the sheep-felon, and flung a running noose of well-soaped round leather (formerly the rein of *Trumpeter*) over his head and down his arms, and then tightened, and turned it, on the backbone of the sheep. "Halloa!" cried Mr. Wenlow; and

"Halloa!" replied Mr. Short; but paused for no further conversation. In a second, he had hitched his running rein, and passed the silk rope of his curtains, round the knees of the man who had invaded his domestic life, and knotted it strictly, in that crampy portion of the human system. Down went Wenlow, with his foul deed on his back, and fouler words issuing vainly from his mouth; which was stopped, by the soft obstruction of a clump of moss, of the *Sphagnum* order.

"To swear is as futile, as it is wrong;" the parson remarked, while he tightened up his knots, and proceeded to add to the embarrassment of his prisoner, by buckling some straps around him. "My friend, you are captured; and your wisest course is, to reconcile yourself to the situation. I don't want to hurt you, more than I can help. There, now you may be quite comfortable."

"I am chok—chok—choking;" the other gasped from out the moss; "if you don't want to kill me on the spot, take that d—d sheep off my neck."

"By no means, my friend. You put him there yourself; and it is not fair to blame him. However, hold up your nose a moment; and

I will give you more room to breathe." With these words, the parson drew forth his own knife, from the sheath at the side of the robber; and smiling at the oddness of the situation, mowed the moss around his prisoner's face; who moved his nose nervously about, from this novel mode of shaving. "My hand is very steady; keep quite still. There now, you will do nicely," continued the vicar; "and can safely express any gratitude you feel."

"I don't feel much;" replied Mr. Wenlow.

"From long experience, I never expect much;" the other answered pleasantly. "But how long, can you stay here, without inconvenience?"

"Either murder me at once; or take that weight off me."

The prisoner uttered this, with such a painful groan, that Mr. Short was really afraid to leave him so, while he went for the needful help to deliver him to justice. Humanely, but unwisely, he relieved him of that burden, while taking good care not to release his arms, or legs. Then, feeling that his fastenings were all secure, and knotted out of reach of any twisting power, the parson sat down to recover his breath (for he had been working nimbly),

as well as to consider, how to carry on his work.
It had been a very hard job to catch this fellow;
and now it seemed a harder one, to dispose of
him, when caught. Here he was, at midnight,
many miles away from any inhabited house
that he knew of; and though the tall man
could have carried him with ease, it was out of
his power, to carry the tall man. If he could
have set him up, to begin with, his head would
have hung upon his hat-crown, like a gurgoyle;
while his heels dragged on the ground, like
the hoppers of a seed-drill. Meditating thus, Mr.
Short, with joy, heard a squeaky little voice, and
beheld Joe Sage. " You are a brave boy," he
said; "and here is a brave job for you." Then
giving him careful directions, and promise of
a crown-piece, if he deserved it, the vicar set
off for a long trudge across the moor.

CHAPTER XI.

MR. ARTHUR, and his guest, Mr. Tucker, sat up, that night, far beyond the usual hour of bed-time, at Lark's cot. When a man begins to tell the story of his life, however concise he may attempt to be, he is pretty sure to wander into many side issues, and get entangled among incidents, that require explanation. The timber-merchant, though accustomed to an early pillow, listened, with scarcely a yawn, to the long, and rather strange, narrative of his host, and made him repeat some parts, to be sure of them; so much at variance did they seem, with the ordinary course of human nature.

"Whether you be right, sir, or whether you be wrong, is not for me to judge," he replied at last; "all dependeth on the thing, that should be uppermost; when two big principles run counter to each other. But whether you be right, sir, or whether you be wrong; there is not a man in fifty thousand, would have done, as you have done."

"I have not been free from doubts myself," his host acknowledged, with a weary sigh; "and that has made it so much harder for me. But now, knowing everything, will you tell me, what you believe to be my first duty?"

"Give me the night, sir, to think it all over; though I don't see, how there can be much doubt about it. But I never heard tell of such affairs before; and things might come across me, like enough, in the night-season; and the head is always clearer, in the morning." The thing, that was coming across the old man, was sleep, heavy sleep; for he had walked far that day, and the change to the Dartmoor air was lulling.

"It is too bad of me, to keep you up so late," Mr. Arthur said, as he looked at his watch. "Good night, my friend; and no dreams of battle. What a poor life it is to dream of!"

After shaking that honest old hand right heartily, the captain sat down, to compose his mind, which was stirred with the many-pronged fork of memory. It was not to please himself, that he had told his tale; but partly that he might not appear mysterious, or churlish, to a trusty friend, and partly because he did really desire advice, in the present see-saw of his fortunes. A strong man scarcely ever takes advice—except in professional questions, or the like—still he may be glad sometimes, to have it, and consider it; even as he would contemplate a pill.

While Mr. Arthur was meditating thus, in the flatness that follows excitement, he heard something soft strike the window behind him, which he had just closed for the night. At first, he took it for the flip of a bat, or perhaps of a Sphinx-moth, attracted by his light; but when it came again, he went, and opened out the lattice; and there he saw a rosebud, upon the sill outside.

"Come down softly," said a voice which he knew well, though forgetting, for a moment, whose it was; "I want to speak to you, without disturbing any one."

Mr. Short made certain that he must be known; but his friend, with a mind intent upon its own affairs, took a big stick before he opened his door; for the outer world was very dark, to eyes contracted by candle-light. "Don't knock me down," Mr. Short said briskly; “I am not a thief—no such luck— only a thief-catcher.”

“Set a thief, to catch a thief,” replied the good man of the house; “but what have you done with him, and what is it about? Come in, and tell me all about it. You are tired; you want something.”

“I never wanted something more, in all my life. Starvation is staring me in the face; and dark as it is, I don’t like her looks. I feel as if I could crunch a bone, after *Nous* had polished it.”

“You shall have as nice a bit of cold salt round, as ever came from Moreton. I was lucky to have it in the house, for we have had an unexpected guest to-day. But he is gone to bed. Is your thief fastened up?”

“I defy him to get away,” replied the hungry vicar; “and even if he does, it is better than to sacrifice a life, so valuable as mine. I spent all my dinner-time, in making springles; and my poor inside has springled me.”

“We will soon cure that,” said Mr. Arthur; “come into the kitchen. It is the best harbour, in a storm of that sort. There now, you can talk, while I fetch the victuals.”

“Erroneous man, you put the cart before the

horse. I will talk, by-and-by. For the present, let me feed. Sweet are the uses of adversity. The next fellow I see, with an empty stomach, shall walk into my larder. Ha, what a draught of ale! Now for the loaf! You might cut that meat, a trifle thicker. Shaving is a waste of time. I can't stop to say, 'thank you.' You will perceive my gratitude, in my proceedings. Three more slices; never mind about the mustard. I never tasted anything so delicious in my life! What a piece of luck, that I saw your candle!"

"And a piece of luck for me," said the hospitable captain; "I was going to bed, perhaps a little in the dumps. I will take a glass of ale myself; and then I am at your service, if there is anything to do."

"There is a lot to do; but I cannot bear to take you from your home, at this time of night. It is simply this—that I have caught, and strapped, and left in the depths of the moor, that fellow who robbed my house, and corded Mrs. Aggett, and stole my grandfather's famous watch. But I don't know, how to bring him down. Like all good-for-nothings, he weighs heavy."

There may have been some jealousy in this

remark ; but the captain was thinking of more urgent matters. " How many miles do you think it is ? And how long is it safe to leave him ? You make a point of having him, I suppose ? "

" I should think I did. About six miles, I should say. But the moor scatters all one's ideas of distance."

" Very well. Then rest yourself, for half an hour. It will be no loss of time ; because the moon will be rising, and then we shall be able to go twice as fast. Meanwhile I will get ready my *feretrum*."

" My very kind friend," said Mr. Short, as he gladly took the offered pipe, and put up his legs to rest a little, " you often use Latin words, rather aptly. Among your other innumerable gifts, that one especially surprises me. For a man, who has knocked about much in the world, forgets straightway every syllable of Latin ; except the examples in his grammar."

" But suppose, that I was brought up for the Church ? Is not the first of all needs, for holy orders, a lively acquaintance with dead languages ? "

" My object is to smoke my pipe in peace. Go you, and get your stretcher ready."

" Upon my word, I believe he was intended for a parson," thought the weary vicar, as he worked his pipe; "and a very good parson has been lost to the world, by some sad mishap; not impossibly a pluck. But they never used to pluck men, in the good old times, half as pluckily as they do now. And the man has brains enough for anything; but for his extraordinary crotchet of manuring the ground with them. However, he is a noble-hearted fellow. Here's to his health, and the increase of such!"

" Now, you can see what a simple thing this is," said his host, returning from the darkness of the door. " I ought to have a patent for it; but—but I don't care. It has cost me a good deal of thought, I can assure you; though you may see nothing worth thinking about. It has these four legs, so that you can rest it. And you fold it up like this; and the legs fold too; and it rides upon your back, as easy as an artist's easel. We have often had 3 cwt. of pot-vines upon it. And here, in case of heavy weight, we can have cross braces. You take them, and I will carry it; in about two minutes, we will set forth. But I must leave a note for my dear Rosie. She will be about, long before we can return; or at any rate, she may be, if anything delays us."

Soon the two sturdy men set forth, with the waning moon lifting an ivory shoulder, like that of Pelops, from the eastern bank of haze. They talked but little; for the way was rough, and the captain's thoughts reverting to his own affairs; of which he said nothing to the parson, having done ample violence already to his habits, by that long narrative to Mr. Tucker. Their course was a winding one, by reason of the ground, and of dark water-beds with bogs among them, so that the pale streak of dawn began to show, below the mounted moon, by the time they reached the Tor. "Shall we knock up old Wisdom in his bed?" asked Mr. Short.

"You know best;" his companion replied. "But I think, it would only be waste of time. We can fetch him out, when we come back; if we want a little change of bearers. You seem very certain, that your man cannot be gone. But I am never sure of anything."

"If he is gone, henceforth I will believe in witchcraft," the vicar answered merrily; "even as my congregation do. Samson himself could not escape such withes."

" Nevertheless, we had better lose no time.
' Fast bind, fast find,' is an excellent proverb,
with a play upon words; such as most of them
have. It was a pity, that you left that boy so
near him."

However, Mr. Short was as cock-sure as ever,
and full of fine faith in his knowledge of
knots. So they strode on vigorously, down the
pastured bottom.

" I could almost have vowed that this must
be the spot," the parson exclaimed at last, with
serious misgivings; " but places are so terribly
misleading, in the dark. It must have been
round the next corner, at the latest." ·

They turned the next corner, and there was
no other, but a long straight reach of open
valley; neither was there any living form in
sight. With a grim look, and a little grinding
of his teeth, Mr. Short led his friend back, to
the bend they had just quitted. " We must
have passed him, among these bushes. It is
simply impossible, that he should have moved.
I defy him to have stirred ten yards;" he
said.

The captain smiled provokingly, for he had
some experience of the way, in which captives
do break loose. " Show me where he is ; I will

put down my hand-barrow. We can find it in a moment, if we find him."

"Of course we shall find him," replied the other; "no sane person can have a doubt about it. He may have rolled a little, as a shot rabbit does; but there is no hole, for him to creep into. Either he has rolled into a clump of furze, or into the bed of the brook. That's it. He has managed to get down to the brook, to drink. How stupid of me, to have overlooked that!"

With certainty renewed, he went back to find him, and searched every tuft of rush, and wet growth; but there was no sheep-stealer there.

"This is the spot where the combat was; and here is the mark where the poor sheep bled," Mr. Arthur called down to him, as the light grew clearer: "but neither sheep, nor man, remains. Is it your opinion, that the sheep rolled too?"

Mr. Short laughed, and said, "You are too right. We are done; that is clear. I never thought about the sheep. If the mutton is gone, so the man must be. What a fool I was, to ease him of his burden so! And he has had the impudence to walk off with it. What an atrocious scoundrel!"

"Well, I rather admire him, for sticking to his purpose. A common rogue would have made off, light-footed. Gone he is, in spite of all your lashings. There can be little doubt, that the boy released him."

"Little Joe Sage! He would never dare to do it. But what is this, stuck upon the furze-bush here? 'Best respects to Rev. Mr. Short, and will return his visit, some fine night.' Upon my word, it becomes too bad! I seem to be made, only to be laughed at."

"Recover your spirits, my dear friend," said the captain, with a lofty endeavour not to smile; "there are times, when all of us have that feeling. But every right-minded person will look grave, at hearing of your trials, and how well you bear them."

"Well, you don't look over-grave, to begin with," complained the poor parson; and then he burst out laughing, wherein Mr. Arthur joined, with freedom of true sympathy.

"It is all very fine for you to laugh," resumed the parson, as if he had not been the aggressor in that vein; "but it is high time to look things in the face. Sheep are a property, unusually sacred in the eye of the law, because so usually stolen. An act of this kind is not to be passed over. When my goods were stolen it was *penes me*, to put up with it in silence, or to make a stir. But when I see another man's sheep made off with, I have no right to sit down, and contemplate the process. I am bound to regard him, with the utmost rigour of the law."

"You have done that already, and a great deal more than that. You have made him fast to his own *corpus delicti*. But you loosed him; and he took his own *habeas corpus*."

"It is too true; there is nothing more stinging, than amiability abused. However, it is not that, that moves me; but the strict compulsion of a simple duty. I shall have to lay the whole of this matter, before the nearest magistrate, Colonel Westcombe; not the nearest to Christowell, but the nearest to the place, where this happened. And I believe he has a kind of shooting-lease, of this very part, where we now stand. So that it would be rude almost, to apply to any other Justice first."

"Certainly it would be. You are quite right." The captain detected, or perhaps imagined, some particles of malice in the parson's words. "If it becomes a matter of business, I am ready to appear, before Colonel Westcombe,

or anybody else, who may be the proper man.
But we must not blame the boy; until we know
a little more about it."

"Boys are a bad lot," said Mr. Short decisively; "they prefer what is nasty to nice
things to talk of; and they would rather do
mischief, than be useful. But I will get it out
of him. Let us be off. Old Sage used to be
a good sort of fellow, enormously conceited;
what I call a fool of wisdom. He knew a great
deal better than Farmer William, the senior
churchwarden, when I spoke well; and everybody looked to him, to nod his head, before they
durst rattle a stick in church. But since he
has been at Okehampton so much, he has heard
some fellows, who preach without a book; and
it seems to have lowered his character. Let
us go, and rout him up, at once. You had
better leave your pot-barrow, to be sent for."

"Not I;" replied the captain, with a good-
tempered smile, for he saw that his valued
friend was cross. "I am not going to have
my invention stolen. The beauty of it is its
portability. Best foot forward; and I am your
man."

When they came to the hut, with the beauty
of the morning resting on the crags above, they

found old John, looking wiser than a thousand Sphinxes, in the fore-front of the hill. "Ah, you gentlemen, gentlemen," he said, "you do looke crule tired surely! I cud a' told 'e, 'twur no good, to go hunting Jack o' lantern. Howsever, I never expects narrabody to harken to me, nowadays."

"Fetch out your little rogue of a grandson;" the vicar demanded sternly.

"Passon, have a care what you be saying," Mr. Sage answered, as he shortened up his braces; "ne'er a one of our vam'ly hath had that name applied to him, without haction, good at law. The poor buy hath been fast aslape all night, in the cornder, behind of me. Did you plaze to think, he were your Jack o' lantern?"

"This beats everything!" exclaimed the parson; while the captain laughed, till he was almost fit to cry; and old John, with amazement, regarded them both.

"'Twor natteral," he said, "to come of so much night-work. You good gentlefolks be pixie-ridden. What a many cases of it I have zeed! My own grandveyther had it dree times, because he were a bit weak-minded. But it comes off easy, when you know the cure. Go you to the biggest stone in sight, and make the cross upon it, and then eat fried bakkon. Her shall be ready, gentlemen, by the time you be; if so be, I can only get little Joe awake, to rout the vire up." Having washed at the spring, he went indoors apace; for he wanted his breakfast also.

CHAPTER XII.

QUO WARRANTO?

"THERE is nothing to be done," said Colonel Westcombe, when Mr. Short had told him the whole of his adventures; " it was your duty, as eye-witness of a felony, to lay an information about it. But after that, you see, we get no further. None of us can say, what this man's name is. We have heard something vague about a warrant being issued, and a good reward offered for his apprehension. But who can apprehend him, when even you have failed? And, if he were taken, he would soon get off. There is not a lock-up that would hold him, in the county; and we could not send him off to London, if that is where he ought to be, without at least three examinations, and remands—supposing that he would stay in custody, so long; which could hardly be expected of him.

But you may feel this, as you go home—which
you shall not do till you have dined with us
—that you have done your utmost, and been
wonderfully near the fulfilment of a public
duty. Although, as I have said, he would
have got off afterwards, by the aid of attorneys,
or the ironmongers. I have had some experience of the Bench already; our intentions are
good, but we do not see our meaning. Whenever he is caught, (as he must be, in the end,)
I hope that it may be beyond us altogether. I
would not discourage you, from laying hands
on him; but, if you can do it, outside our
division, it would be a much better thing for
everybody."

"And that is your settled conclusion, is it?
That, because a man is hard to catch, we must
not attempt to catch him! If your practice
with the Frenchmen had been such, what a
thorough thrashing you would have got!"

"Of course we should," the colonel answered;
"and thoroughly deserved it too. But there
never will be such a set of men again. There
are no such fellows, in the commission of the
peace."

"If you consider it the right thing, to be
beaten by a rogue, because you have none but

fools to help you; there is nothing more for me to say, Colonel Westcombe."

"Now don't be so peppery, my dear friend," said the colonel, offering an easy chair; "if there is anything you can suggest, sit down, and talk over it quietly. Everybody knows your abilities, Short. You must not imagine that because they have made me a 'beak,' as it is called, I set myself up, to lay down the law, to a clever man like you. I know nothing whatever of the law, any more than the rest of the J.P.'s do. We try to act, according to the light of common sense. And what more can you expect of us?"

"Certainly, nothing beyond common sense. We are glad that you should have it—possibly, as a new gift of office. But is it common sense, that a neighbourhood, however wild, and thinly peopled it may be, should be harassed for months, by a desperate fellow, simply because he is desperate? And that you, with your stern sense of discipline, my friend, should put up with it, and make excuses for it!"

"Well, I don't like it. And I may be doing more than you know of, to try to put a stop to it. Whose sheep was it, that was killed, and stolen? He should come, and sign a deposition."

"The sheep affair is nothing, in comparison with the rest. Are we all to be sheep, and have our throats cut, at the first convenience of that villain? How much longer, till you do something?"

"That depends mainly upon circumstances," replied the colonel blandly; "drum-head law will not do here. There is some informality about the warrant; if what I was told, the other day, is true. The coroner issued his warrant first, somewhere in Surrey, or in Bucks, perhaps it was. And after that, the magistrates issued theirs; and both of them were wrong, they seem to say. However, that is not in any way my business; and I have heard a dozen stories, as to what his name is. If I could have my own way, my plan would be to treat him as a brigand, hunt him down, and then hand him over to the civil authorities, with a double twist of tent-rope, round his moving members. But such things are not to be done, in this age."

"I fear that we are tumbling all to pieces now;" said Mr. Short, trying to be brisk about it; "I am not at all a stickler for the fine old times; but I do like a little bit of decency. When a man shows any sign of real wit, I can make over-much allowance for him; for the chuckle in his brain upsets his sense. But look at this thing, written here in pencil; there is no wit in it, only vulgar insolence."

"You could scarcely expect," replied the colonel, examining the paper found upon the furze-bush; "that a man's jocosity should be at its best, when he has been strapped up for some hours. But I call this very fair; not strikingly facetious perhaps, but civil, and well-worded. And it shows good will, to a limited extent. Come, come, we must not be too hard upon him. I never did believe that story, about his murdering two women. Look! The man spells every word correctly, at any rate so far as I can judge; and I have had some experience in that, though I left school very early. Do you mean to tell me, Short, that any man would murder two women, who could spell like that, on the spur of the moment, and by a lantern?"

"A' maight, and yet again a' maightn't; as our Farmer William says;" Mr. Short was not going to add to his troubles an argument, on so abstruse a point. "I suppose he has let your grouse alone?"

Colonel Westcombe was too good to suppose, that his friend could mean, by that last remark, any paltry insinuation. " I don't know whether he has, or not," was all he said about it.

" Well now," continued the vicar, who ought to have been more ashamed than he actually was; " I want to know, what you make out of those letters, or half-letters, here at the top of the paper. You see that this paper has been torn off, probably after being doubled down, from a sheet of something—perhaps a letter. The crease, which has guided the severance, was meant, most likely, to have come beneath the last line of the letter; but instead of that, it happens to have taken the last line, pretty nearly along its belt; as one might say. We have the lower half of the words still here; in some places more, and in some parts less; for the writing is not, to a nicety, straight, though more so than happens, in nine cases out of ten. Can you make out, what these words have been ? "

" Not I," replied the colonel; " 'tis as much as I can do, to make out words, when I get them in the lump. I could not read even print, bisected. And, if this is a private communication, what right have we to exert our brains upon it ? "

" Every possible right, against such a villain; to protect society from him. I have spared no labour to decipher that bisected line; and I am pretty sure that I have done so; although there are some words still uncertain. With the upper half, it would have been much easier work; still I think that I have made the words out— ' to remove her, at one day's notice. But beware of harming her.' And the signature, in the same line with it, was either Y. Y. or G. G.— What mischief is this fellow up to next?"

"Whatever it is, I shall be much obliged to him, if he will do it on your side of the moor. Over in Bovey Tracy, and Moreton, and Newton, there are magistrates of long magisterial descent, who understand wicked ways, and the way to deal with them. But here, there is nobody to give me the lead, or even to back me up, if I should take it. And everybody wants me to put down everybody else, because I have been accustomed to fight the French. It is quite another pair of shoes, I can tell you."

"Of course it is, and they do not fit you; however, you will trudge on, till they do. You have the right stuff for it; good will, common sense, activity, and the love of justice. You will be the best Justice in the county, after two or three years of experience, and the most

popular, and the most respected one; because
of your upright, and generous nature."

" You ought to be more consistent, Short;
you were running me down, not two minutes
ago."

" And so I will, when it is necessary; for I
give every man his due, be it praise or blame.
But without going into that, what does this line
mean?   I make something serious of it."

" If you can make head, or tail of it, although
it is all tail already, you ought to be chief-
constable of the county."

" A man who can't catch his own thief!
However, by the light of imagination, I do
make some tail of it.   My interpretation is, that
these rogues mean to carry off Rose Arthur."

Colonel Westcombe looked at Mr. Short, with
intense, yet rational amazement. " I have known
you make wonderful hits," he said; " and the
cleverest woman in Okehampton says, that you
have beaten her thoroughly. Still, you must
have something more to show, than this broken
line, before you speak like that."

" Certainly, I have other things to go by;
and I will tell you what they are. I have not
spoken about them sooner; because my friend
Arthur had his reasons—which are quite un-

known to me—for holding aloof from your good
worship. But since you have found him out,
and met him, my restriction vanishes. I mean,
that I am at liberty to mention him to you;
which I could not properly do before. Very
well; I know, though I have not told him of it,
that this infamous fellow, whoever he may be—
has been prowling, more than once, about his
place; although there are no sheep there to
steal, neither is his house worth robbing. Also
I know, from two or three things, which I have
picked up, in hunting out my own grievance,
that he has done this, at the instigation of
another fellow, perhaps even worse than himself. Therefore, I begin to smell a rat."

"I never could see into a complication," the
colonel replied, with his honest face quite red,
for he had taken a great liking to Miss Arthur;
"I always look at men, as if they were like me."

"That is the worst of being honest. You are
almost sure to make that mistake. And poor
Arthur makes it also, and will probably have to
pay for it. He believes entirely in a stupid
fellow, who means no harm, I dare say; but
means his own good, first of all. The fellow
relies on his thickness; like a crocodile letting
down his eyelids. But he sees a deal more,

than he pretends to see; and Betty Sage tells me, that he has been and bought a red-cushioned chair, to go to sleep in. It follows, that he must have had a tip; and where would he get it, without treachery? He never comes to church, and he doesn't send his children. They are becoming a nest of savages, at Brent-fuzz corner, where he lives. I have told Arthur, that it is his duty, to make his workmen come to church; but he told me, that he never meddled with such matters."

" I think that he was quite right," replied the colonel; " he might try to persuade them; as I do with mine. Anything more is beyond his business. They resent it; and in their place, we should do the same."

" That is true enough; and I have not pressed it. Still, the fellow used to come to church; and he sleeps enough for two, in the week-days. Our schoolmaster used to have to knock him on the head, on account of the snoring noise he made; and that was sometimes undesirable. But it roused up the others; and in his absence, old Jacobs, who must be doing something with his rod, has given offence, by administering a rap to men, who are considerable ratepayers. And that makes us miss Sam Slowbury."

"I can understand that. But reflect a moment, Short. May not the want of this outlet for the stick have created some prejudice, in your mind, against the man?"

"Not in the least. It has only induced me to consider his evil ways. And I do not dwell upon these large points only. But the other day, I came upon him, round a corner, in the thick of my friend's plantation. And instead of being fast asleep, he was standing up, staring as if he had just seen a ghost. 'What's the matter, Sam?' I said; and *Nous*, who was with me, pelted away, in full hunt of some enemy. Sam could not answer; but his eyes were jumping, like peppercorns, in a mill, going to be ground. He wanted to look at me; and he wanted to look after the vanished one; and also after *Nous*; and most of all, he wanted to be looking nowhere. So I spoke again; and I said, 'Sam, the Devil hath got hold of thee.' When he heard those words, he laid hold of a tree; and you might have heard his heart go thumping. 'Make a clean breast of it, Sam,' I exhorted him, in my deepest pulpit-voice; and he gurgled in his throat, and was trying to fetch words; when back comes that confounded *Nous*. You know, what the training of that dog is. When he has anything particular to say, or any excuse to urge for his failures, he sits up, and begs, like a little lap-dog. Well, he came, and sat up in that ludicrous style, between Sam Slowbury and me; and the whole of Sam's conscience was gone, in a second. I never felt more put out with *Nous*. I know it was unjust—you need not tell me. But there was a sort of crisis; and he had undone it. I shall never get such an opportunity again. Before I could recover my condition to go on with it, Slowbury was grinning, with a fine red face, and all his little budget of wits come back."

"And a little budget will beat a big one, Short," said the colonel, who enjoyed his friend's upset; "I have seen that, a hundred times; and I have done it myself, sometimes, with the clever people. Not that I could ever do it, with you though, my friend. Keep out of the range of the rifle-men."

"It is a trifle altogether," continued the vicar, "that I should be laughed at, through the sheer force of circumstances—which have been most sadly against me of late—by a disloyal member of my parish, who was just reduced properly to his marrow-bones. I care not two skips of a flea for that; because I must collar him, by-and-by. I trust in the justice of my cause, and the coal and blanket club; to which he must pay up seven shillings' and sixpence, or lose fifteen. I shall have him full of piety, by All Saints' Day; but the pest is to have lost the clean breast he was making. I could not help giving *Nous* a smack, for his absurdity."

"Then you ought to have had it yourself," said his friend; "but what do you suppose you would have heard from Sam? You have such a gift of putting things together, that you must know, (almost as well as if you had heard it) what had happened to him."

"He had given audience to some rogue; perhaps this very villain who has robbed me of my watch, and who wants to have his turn with Arthur. Why should *Nous* have set off, like that, unless he smelled a well-known enemy? A common tramp, or a workman on the lounge, would never have stirred him up like that. He recognized some one who had wronged him, by his scent, and probably pursued him, till he crossed the stream."

"You will lose your favourite," replied Colonel Westcombe; "unless he controls his feelings better. That man will kill him, if they meet again. But why have you not given Mr.

Arthur warning, of this dangerous fellow prowling round his place? That seems to me the first thing, you should have done."

"With an ordinary man, it would have been so. And even in his case, I have doubted. But he lives a peculiar life, and detests any interference, or suggestion. Also I have felt that, without more proof, I might do a great wrong to Slowbury, who has a large family, depending on his wages. Therefore I resolved to wait a little, and endeavour myself to intercept the danger. And now, I shall be glad of your advice."

"I believe, that you have acted aright so far. Wisely, I mean, as well as justly. But what to do next—I must have time to think." Here the colonel began to move his thick grey eyebrows, as he always did, to aid grave mental process. "In the first place, it cannot be the desire of the law, that such a fellow should go on defying it, for ever. Sarcastic as you are, you can hardly maintain, that such would be the desire of the law."

"One would scarcely think so; unless one judged the law, by its actions. And that would not be fair; because it does not judge us so."

"Very well; let us take that for granted.

Assuming then, as we may safely do, that the law would like to catch that man, how are we to carry out its wishes? I am told, that it would take at least a company of soldiers, not such fellows as they have now, but really disciplined, and seasoned men, to surround his haunts, and work him out. He shifts his quarters, according to the weather, and the time of year, and the condition of his health, which must upon the whole be strong; or surely he would be laid up with ague. How he escapes it, I cannot understand."

" He must be doubled up with rheumatism, if it were not for the frequent change of air, and the constant use of this specific." Here Mr. Short showed Colonel Westcombe the cover of a pill-box, which he had found near the place of his conflict with the felon; and his friend knew immediately what it was, and shook his head sadly, that the rogue should be so clever.

" He may live in the bogs for weeks together, if he has plenty of those," said the colonel; " I wish I could get my young grouse to take them; for I fear they find the climate damp. But now, about this villain—if indeed he is a villain; for I hear that he entertains a high regard for me, though he has not extended it to you, my friend—it appears to me, that we must not be rash, but first get a new warrant from head-quarters; which would prove that we are in earnest; and then put our heads together, how to execute it. I don't know this matter right out, at present. As Jack used to say, when he was at Oxford, ' I haven't got it up; ' though he never broke down, because he is blest with such ability. But from what I hear, he was first to be arrested, upon the warrant of the coroner; and when that came to nothing, some jealousy arose; and I don't know exactly, how it was. However, there seems to be a warrant now flourishing; only I am told that the name is wrong. However, I shall see a man on Tuesday fortnight, who will be able to tell us more about it. And then, we shall be able to take some steps."

"But how many steps will he have taken? My dear friend, you used not to be like this. Did you wait, till Tuesday fortnight, when the enemy was in front of you ? "

"Not we. But that was quite a different thing. We understood what we were at. But now, I must tell you candidly, that I don't know." Then the colonel laughed; and the parson did the same.

"It is all very fine to laugh," resumed the latter; "but the thing is no joke, after all. It seems to be a lucky thing, that he got away; or you might have committed me, for an assault. I shall take good care, not to risk my life again; if this is the proper course of justice. But who is our great authority, who will set things straight, in three weeks' time?"

"My old friend, General Punk, has promised to be with us, for the shooting then. Of course, you will join us, and bring *Nous*. Now you need not smile; for the general has promised to go to the authorities, and put things straight. It is useless to beat about the bush like this. I feel the reproach of it, as much as you do. And the very first instant, when I see my way ——"

"The truth of it is," said Mr. Short, "that the brigands, and the soldiers, were hand in glove in Spain; and you love, and admire, the whole tribe of them."

CHAPTER XIII.

THE SILVER KEY.

WHILE these things thus were going on, or to put it more correctly, sticking fast, the people, concerned about them in London, were getting into active ways. Mrs. Giblets, and her daughter Mary, now went out along the streets, and across them too, almost as calmly, as if it had been Northernhay. Finding no harm come of this, they began to despise both road, and pavement; till the widow of Barnstaple's mayor, at last, took to hitching up her dress, and holding up her hand, and putting a stop to the public conveyances, as often as fancy impelled her to see, what that shop over the way was. In a word, they treated our vast metropolis, as if their own family had built it.

"Only you mind one thing, Mary," Mrs. Giblets used to say, before she tied her bonnet-strings; "if any man asketh you the way to

this part, or to thiccy; you look at him, as if
you knew, but refused to hold discourse with
him. It is the commonest trick they have, for
finding out where you come from; and then
they get you down an alley; and your friends
may put you in the paper." To which Mary
always made reply, " Not they, mother. Have
no fear for me; 'twould take a deep one to best
me now. You ask Aunt Snacks, what I said to
the tea-fishman. If ever you saw a man look
astonished——"

" He won't be the only one, my dear. We
shall astonish more than him, before we get
back to Exeter."

For now Mrs. Giblets had strict orders from
her brother, to leave no stone unturned, in
tracing the intentions of the red-faced man.
There had been some counsel, between Mr.
Arthur, and his good friend, the timber-merchant; wherein, Mr. Tucker, having keen ap-
preciation of the great human final cause, £ s. d.,
urged upon his host the expediency of going,
to look after that same in London. However,
it is not an easy thing, to break the habitude
of years, and the sense of peace; and beyond
that, the captain had good reason, for not quit-
ting home just now. His foremost duty, and

entire love, bound him to his daughter there.
And to leave her, in that lonely house, or to put
her elsewhere, or to take her with him, would
all be either bad, or doubtful. Moreover, he
had his own proud dislike, of making any
overture to his father, after all that had passed
between them; and he felt that the hand which
had driven him away, should be held out to
him, before he rushed to take it. Therefore,
he refused to go to London.

But an agent is often more impulsive than
his principal; and so was Mr. Tucker now. To
him it appeared a burning shame, that rogues
should be left to work their will, through
magnanimous neglect. On the captain's behalf,
and with his leave, he resolved at least to watch
the case, and keep him informed of urgency.
And to help him, he could scarce have found
a better ally, than the enterprising Snacks.

That gentleman's conduct was not wholly un-
tainted by self-interest. He had the privilege of
knowing Messrs. Powderhorn and Bullrush, the
solicitors for the railway company, whose hot
haste had been so impeded, by the crotchety
old earl. With the arrogance of all railway-
lawyers, they had taken it quite as a personal
affront, that their powers of compulsory pur-

chase should meet with even a moderate demur. To overbear all such small nonsense, was their manner, with small men. But a great land-owner, like the earl, was not to be overborne so gaily; and there were some informalities about their plans, and notices, which might throw them over for another twelvemonth, if keenly sifted, by big-fee'd counsel. Therefore they hated the earl, as if he had rushed into their office—which the gout, alas, prevented—and submitted to them, for counsel's opinion, a vigorous kick at every acting partner. Being aware of this perhaps unworthy, but certainly natural sentiment, Mr. Snacks saw his way to getting a grateful allotment, below market-figures; if he could only succeed in putting a big spoke into the bad earl's wheel. So that he shared the tender interest of his Devon-shire visitors, in the gloomy, and rather lonely mansion, standing within those ivied walls.

If any man wants to get into a house, where he has no right to be, let him set feminine wits at work, and defy them to accomplish it. It does not follow, that he will get in himself; but the better one will do so, and tell him all she sees; which is certain to be far beyond his sight. And good Mrs. Snacks, being stirred

up thus, resolved that the mistress of three
husbands should never be beaten, by a stupid
lot of maids, who understood nothing but the
way to bang the door.

If there were time, it might seem worth
while, to tell how this lady did get in; after
carefully watching all the bays of wall, to be
certain where the run might best be made.
But although it was a noble exploit, who but
she can tell the tale? And there is not room
to let her do it; because the largeness of her
mind embraces a family of fifty narratives,
during the production of a single one. Enough
it is to say, that some very honest fellow, who
supplied the premises with something large—
whether it were milk, or oil, or ale,—was persuaded to consider half-a-crown so long, that
he set down his cans against the spring-door
in the wall; and Mrs. Snacks, quite overcome
with the heat of the day, slipped in, and
fainted. Being still unmarried, this man became alarmed, for Mrs. Snacks was of considerable size; and he hurried to the house, and
called out maids; in pursuance of whom, came
the housekeeper; a truly pretentious, and excellent woman, married into the name of
"Tubbs." At first, Mrs. Tubbs was inclined

to be haughty, and to fetch the gardener, and
a groom, and send the invader to the nearest
chemist's shop.   But as soon as she saw a
magnificent gold chain, peeping through the
sick lady's mantle, and six fine rings upon
the poor limp fingers, the noblest feelings of
humanity were touched, and she whispered the
sad words—" Cholera, syncope, collapse, I fear!
Sir John says, that it is not infectious.   Don't
be frightened, you stupid girls.   Bring the
poor dear, to my downstairs room.   Luckily,
Mr. Gaston is from home.   We are not quite
savages, I should hope.   Stuff!   If you won't
help to carry her, I will."

Mrs. Tubbs knew a good deal of medicine,
and kept certain antidotes of her own ; which
she longed to try first upon somebody else.
And so efficacious were these, that Mrs. Snacks,
submitting, like a martyr, to the palatable
parts, comprising very old cherry-brandy, was
able to sit up, in three-quarters of an hour,
and confessed to a genial glow, throughout her
system.

" How sad it does seem, that we should be
such poor things!" she whispered, through
her tears, to her kind preserver ; " but without
that, how should we ever know the warm

hearts from the cold ones? I suppose, that we all adhere to life; even when best prepared to go. And in my case, it would have been so sad; because of my husband, who adores me, and my child, who has such lofty expectations. Oh, Mrs. Tubbs, shall I live long enough to thank you?"

"I trust that you will, ma'am; if you take another glass. Your colour has come back most charming. I was very near sending for Sir John Tickell, his lordship's own doctor; but you looked up at me, out of symptoms, so confiding. And you see, he could not have done much more."

"Nor a quarter so much, dear Mrs. Tubbs. I shall always declare that you saved my life. It came all across me, in such a sudden way; and you understood it, in a moment!"

"That I did, ma'am; from keeping my eyes open. What else can I do, in such a house as this? But there! I mustn't trouble you, with our affairs."

"It seems to be a sort of institution. It struck me in that light, before my seizure; and I just had the sense, to think it safer than the street. But little could I dream of such skill within."

"'Tis a queer sort of institution, ma'am. However, it is not my place to talk; and talk I never do, not to my own sister, though her husband is a tanner in Bermondsey."

"Mrs. Tubbs, you are quite right. People are so apt to pry; and gossip is so hateful. In all my life, I never could abide it, and shut myself out of many doors, through that. You may know what I am, when I tell you, that although we have a nice house, with bow windows, looking right over the Regency Park, it never hath come into my mind, to ask whose institution this was here. I look out of my windows, and my neighbours may look in; but as for a desire to look into theirs, the mere idea of a thought about it hath never been known to come into my mind."

"Excuse me, ma'am," Mrs. Tubbs replied, with a new light of interest kindling in her eyes; "but if I may make so bold, did you happen to come from the West of England?"

"From the west, and the best of the west," said Mrs. Snacks, who could tell what Mrs. Tubbs was; "my father lived at Crediton, all his life; and my brother was the Mayor of Barnstaple."

"I am not Devonshire, so to speak; or not altogether that, and that only," Mrs. Tubbs answered, with her finger-tips meeting, while she thought the subject out; "but my father was of very excellent parentage, in Somerset; and my dear mother, who I lost without the knowledge, came away direct, in early days, from a substantial house at Appledore. And if we can only find the papers, and my good husband comes up again,—which he generally does, at about three years, because he is a seafaring man,—the best authorities agree, that no one will be able to keep us out of it. Perhaps you have heard of the matter, ma'am— West Boddlebury farm, near Appledore?"

"Of course, I have, over and over again. But my husband is the one, who understands those things; and we have very influential friends near there. Some of them are at our house now; come to see London, and spend their money. If you could manage to come, and see us, and have a bit of early dinner with us, as they do in Devonshire, my husband, who is an extraordinary man, might thank you for saving my life, or at least prolonging it— although I feel a little queer again—and you might gain some information, of the greatest value to you."

"Looking at you sitting there, ma'am," said

Mrs. Tubbs, who had thought it prudent to take some disinfectant fluid, " with your fine west-country colour, such as London burns away, thinking of what you might have been in an hour, as our fishmonger was, bluer than his own mackerel fish ; it do seem to me, to have been a providence, that the side-walk door was open. We have a great gentleman here, who is the master's master, as the saying goes, and keeps the household most select. None of the lower ones can get out ; and he would like to keep me boxed up too. But I went to my lord, when I knew that he was in one of his kicking tempers ; and I said—' My lord, is it your orders, that I am to be locked in here, after all the years that I have served you ? ' And he roared out—' Tubbs shall go where she likes. Tubbs has my orders to go, when she pleases, to '——not at all a nice place, ma'am, which I will not offend you by speaking of, though patronized by the nobility. And ever since that, I have made a point of taking my walk in the park, of a Sunday, and looking about for sailors' hats ; for my husband must come home some day, and perhaps with a pocket full of money. For the Lord, He doeth all things well."

" Indeed He does," Mrs. Snacks replied ; " my husband knows all about the shipping, and he has some connection with the Docks. Then Mrs. Tubbs, we shall expect you, at two o'clock next Saturday. We generally have a turbot first, with Aylesbury ducks, and marrowfats, to follow. But perhaps that would not be to your taste. In these large establishments, you live so well."

" Not at all, ma'am, not at all. We are kept very close here, I can tell you. We lead a very assceltic life ; and have not even seen a lamb's fry yet."

" Then, my dear Mrs. Tubbs, we shall expect you. Here is my card, and our gate is never locked. Or shall we send the carriage for you ? No, you prefer to be independent. And I will follow your example. I will just slip out, and get a cab, before that formidable man comes back. He might consider me an intruder ; and that would be unpleasant to you, I can see."

" My dear lady," exclaimed Mrs. Tubbs, " I am not one, to be lorded over, by a man no better than myself. It has been going on too long. I never speak of private matters. But you will not blame me, when I come to see you,

if I should make bold to consult you a little,
concerning my own position, which is a trial
beyond my mind, at times."

Accordingly, when this faithful person,
punctual to her hour on Sunday, had made a
pre-eminent dinner, and admired the view of
a crowd in the park (who might be taken, thus
far off, for London trees walking off their
woes), and then had refused more Frontignac—
a wine that has now gone the way of all fashion
—because she was determined to consider slowly
what Mr. Snacks had said, about investment,
when she happened to confess that she had
put by, in spite of hard times, just a little bit
of money; and when she had been persuaded,
as a favour, to everybody present, and especially her host, to relent from that refusal, and
touch flower-bells with Mr. Snacks (who was
an exceedingly pleasant man), really such a
desire to please those, who had pleased her so
much, became established in her kind heart,
that Mrs. Giblets, and Mrs. Snacks, and even
Mary—although she was ordered to run away
three times, and so lost three half minutes,
before she ventured back again—one with
another, putting things together, could enter
into all the affairs of that interesting house,

almost as clearly, as if they had the privilege of
living there.

To put into a few words a story which cost
many, the present Earl Delapole, although by
nature of haughty and imperious vein, in his
later years had fallen deeply under the influence
of a man, who had made his way upward from
post to post. From the position of farm-bailiff,
and rent-collector's deputy, upon a small part
of the earl's estates, he had risen to be the
general agent, steward, manager, and master.
There still were times, when the rightful lord,
who was of a very suspicious mind, would
rebel, break out most violently, and order his
enemy to quit his sight, and his premises, for
ever. At such times, Mr. Gaston used to fling
out of the house, and bang the door; but the
next day, he was back again, having made
himself indispensable; all that violence only
tightened the noose, as with a well-set wire.
Mrs. Tubbs could not say, whether she considered him a rogue, or not; perhaps, if he had
not been so boisterous, and so domineering, she
would have thought him deficient in principle;
but she had never known a rogue, with a voice
so loud, and a face so red.

The earl, being now in his eightieth year,

was falling, more and more completely, into the power of this tyrant. No one ever came to brighten his dulness, or divert his mind towards any kind of charity; although he must have a mint of money, in land, and houses, and leather bags. Mr. Gaston would take good care of that. Only his doctor, Sir John Tickell, who always went about with a trumpet—which perhaps was make-believe, because he hated questions—and his lawyer, Mr. Latimer, though even he seemed to be shut out now, and his shaver (who could not be shut out); these were all that were let in now, with any sort of grace about it. If any old gentleman, who had carried on highly, in the fine old times, with his lordship, desired to shake him by the hand once more, and to lighten it up for him to hold on, and to say things witty, as they used to be —there was no other message, when his card came in, but that his lordship was in great pain to-day. And so, the very best of them dropped off; gentlemen, who must have been the foremost of their day, in carrying on high wickedness. Mrs. Tubbs liked them, because they were gentlemen; not such soft-mouths, as you see now. But although she liked them, and they liked her (as their compliments on her appearance proved), she durst not authorize man, or maid, to show them up to his lordship's room. And this had grown sadly upon the earl; quite according to Mr. Gaston's wishes; ever since the grandson died, following that poor lord his father, who had never been much to speak of. However, it was known among the older ones, that there was another son somewhere, or at any rate there used to be; but the earl had refused to have him mentioned, because of some trouble that he had been through. And although he might forgive him now, for the sake of the land, and the title, Mrs. Tubbs was sure, that Mr. Gaston would give him no chance of repentance.

"That is how things always goes, with our great families;" said Mr. Snacks, a liberal of the largest order, who liked the world to go up and down. "Men who think, that nothing less than a coach and four, of their own driving, is fit to come through their property. Their time is pretty well up, on this earth. But the son, if there is one, should be looked up; to make a good title to the company."

Through the caution of the timber-merchant,

none of those present knew, that the missing
son could be found on Dartmoor; though some
of them began to suspect it.

"But if these troubles go on much longer,
what am I to do?" asked the good housekeeper,
who felt that she might have unburdened her
mind, to bring worse burden afterwards; "I
can throw up my situation, of course; and
goodness knows, it is a gloomy one."

"No, ma'am, no!" exclaimed Mr. Snacks;
"you must not contemplate such a step. For
the good of the family, you must not do that.
You are so placed, that an immensity depends
upon your discretion, and forbearance. To-
morrow is Monday. I will feel my way, towards
getting you those shares we spoke of. If I
succeed, as I fully hope to do, your money will
be doubled by Friday morning. My invest-
ments are never speculative; but sound as the
Bank of England. I will not say a syllable,
to disturb your mind. Cast off every thought
about it. I shall act for you, with even more
discretion, than I should employ about my own
affairs. And I think I can promise you another
thing. From my intimate acquaintance with
the Docks, I shall have the pleasure of telling

you next Sunday, if you most kindly repeat your visit, the latitude, and longitude of Captain Tubbs; and perhaps the very day when he must come home, after making all allowance for wind, and weather."

This brought a very nice smile into the eyes of the house-keeping lady, who was not so very old; and if Mr. Gaston could have seen, how warmly, and gratefully, she wished her new friends good-night, perhaps it would have made him grind his teeth, and hesitate about his next proceeding.

CHAPTER XIV.

UNDER THE ASH-TREE.

THE evening of a ripe summer day was slanting down the western heights, and spreading waves of peace and rest (too soft to be called shadows yet), along the fertile lowland, and the villages, where people talk. The striped proceedings of the harvest, and the winding tree-girt roads, and meadows coned with hay, uncarted still (because of summer-floods), patches also, streaked according to the coat they had put on (whether of beans, or rape, or turnips, or the hungry and hungrifying potato, or brown vetches spent in pods), and the green leisure of soft pasture, frilled with alders by the brook—these, and a thousand other beauties, spreading wide content to gaze at, lay in the mellow summer eve, below the rampart of rough moor.

Returning from Christowell, in time to get her father's supper ready, Rose, with one hand full of wood-bine, blue-cup, and dark beads of worts, espied a lovely place to rest in, and enjoy the varied view. A bend of the wandering lane lay open, where a gate had once kept guard; for time had dispersed the gate; and man, and his cattle, had dispensed with it. Over the moss-browed granite posts, (whose heads were antlered, like a stag's,) a grand old ash-tree, hung with tassels, spread a cool awning, to improve the sight. Ferns, and fox-gloves, and puce heath-flowers, fringed the descent of the steep fore-ground; while the low-land distance wavered with the slowly gliding shades of hill.

Here she sat, to think a little of the beauties earth presents, and perhaps (although she was so young) of the many troubles it inflicts. She was capable—as she thought—of putting two and two together; but this capability had not brought the comfort of so rare a gift. Nothing came of meditations; and perhaps the wisest plan would be, to stop them altogether. But this was easier said, than done; none but the most commanding minds can turn their pressure off and on ; and Rose was not given to pry con-tinually into her own machinery.

The sweetness of the hovering light, and calm

of summer fragrance, were enough to make one think of nice things here, and scorn anxiety. Far in the distance people clearly were at work, but made no noise; and nearer toward, at the hill-foot, cows (as quiet as the milky way) jotted the winding meadows, with slow movement, seeking the prime of dew. There was nothing to disturb one's mind, under the dignity of that tree; unless the disturbed one brought it with him, or let himself be vexed (through excess of sensibility), by the lightly mended fractures, which the Christow made a murmur of. In defiance of breakage, the brook flowed on; in erasure of shadows, the evening spread; and over the lines of care and trouble, the young heart passed into the like repose.

There could not have been a better time, for any one to look at her, with her head reclined against the granite pier, and her hat full of flowers by her side. The rugged face of the stone set off the delicate damask of her own, and the hoary lichens, of a hundred years, made a foil for the brightness of silky young locks. It was doubtful, whether she was half-asleep, or wholly thinking; but in either case, a gentle smile was sweetly resting with her. And not to disturb its beauty, or his own delight in watching it, a young man (who had come softly up the turfy slope) drew back, and pondered.

By some strange gift of time, and place, this happened to be John Westcombe, who had long been in a condition of mind, more easy to feel, than to describe. It had neither been distraction, anguish, transport, misery, temerity, abasement, nor any of the many dark profundities of despair. Rather, there had been, from time to time, some element of all those moods, combining undesirably, and confounding self-inspection. And now to see the cause of all this stir, intensified it. For since that day at Fingle-bridge, he had only seen her far away, although he had diligently fished the river, to the utmost of his privilege. "This is a fair chance now," thought he, "on neutral ground—the Queen's highway, or at any rate, a parish road. Am I to go on like this, for ever, until some dishonourable fellow cuts me out? How sweetly lovely she does look! There never was any one like her."

For her simple dress, long-waisted, flowing (and neither skewered in, nor scrimped to show a foot squeezed into a lobster's claw, nor thatched with stripes of hideous hues) followed the elegance of her form; as nature's self would have

provided, if the human race were born in husks,
as a comely filbert is. The finish of every part
was perfect, like a sculptor's dream (but happily
quite unlike his deeds), from the tapering finger-
tips, and nails, resembling the aforesaid filbert,
to the carven curves, and flexured tracery of
soft little ears, that had never been bored. To
these Jack Westcombe thought it now good time
to make his love's appeal.

"You did not know that I was here. I came
up, quite by accident. And I hope you won't
be angry with me, for—for looking at you?"

"After all your kindness, how could I be
angry with you, for—for looking at me?"

"But I want to do a good deal more than
that. I want to tell you, if I may, the continual
things I think of you. You cannot understand
them; but I should like to make them clear to
you."

"But how can you do that, if they are beyond
my understanding?"

"Not at all," said Jack; "if you will only
try to put yourself in my place. Suppose that
you loved anybody, with all your heart, and
for all your life. The first thing you would
want to do, would be to make it clear to
them."

" But they would be sure to know it. Why should I tell them, what they knew already? They would feel, that I was doing it."

" Then do you feel, that I am doing it, doing it ever more, for you? And if you do, are you vexed about it ? "

Rose had risen, and was looking at him, with maiden bashfulness, and some grief. " You are not thinking what you say ; " she said.

" Yes, I am. I have thought about it, for days, and nights, and weeks, and months. Ever since I first saw you, nothing else has been really in my thoughts. I cannot expect you to care for me yet ; but only say, that you will try. Put it in this way to yourself. Say, ' here is a fellow not worth much, and in no single way to be compared to me. But he loves me, with all his heart and soul ; and lovely as I am, I never shall get any body else, to do it half so well.' "

" Really, Mr. Westcombe, if I am to talk to myself like that, I must be a mass of self-conceit."

" So you ought to be. And then, go on like this—' although I don't care about him now, and he does not come up at all to my ideas, it is my duty to give him fair play, and not for a

moment to entertain a single thought of any
other person; until I have tried my very best
to like him.' Now, will you promise to consider
it like that ? "

" Surely your ideas of fair play," she answered,
with a smile of pleasure at his skill in putting
things, so as not to terrify her, " are fairer to
yourself, supposing that—that you make a point
of me, than they are to any other person; such
as I am not to think of."

" How can I argue with you," said Jack,
contriving to get very near to her, without
any perceptible nearing, " unless you could
spare me your hand, that I might count my
reasons on it ? "

" I am afraid, that I ought to go home; " said
Rose.

" Thank you for being afraid ; " he answered,
with much ability offering his hand, in the
manner of one who says, ' Good-bye ; ' " because
it seems almost to mean, that you are not afraid
to be with me. It seems almost, as if you were
beginning at last to understand, just a little, how
I worship you."

" Hush ! You must not use such words. It
is quite sinful. You may say ' love ' me.
But——"

"Oh, if you give me leave to say 'love you,' I shall care for nothing more. Come, you can never call that back."

"But I have given you no leave at all! You are taking the whole of it, yourself," said Rose, as he began to count her fingers, in one of the many bedazements of love, as mothers count the baby's toes—"Good-night, and good-bye, was the leave you were to take. And if you won't do it, I must do it for you."

"I am off, at once. Or at least I shall be off, before you can count ten. Only before I go, be so very kind, as to do me one little favour. You know that I am not unreasonable?"

"I have always thought that of you, until—till now."

"I will do my best, for you to think it still. I ask you nothing more than this—to give me both your hands, and say—'John Westcombe, I will think kindly of you.'"

"Why those are the very words Sam Slowbury says, that his wife used to him; and whenever they quarrel, he reminds her of them."

"I shall be quite content to be reminded of them, fifty thousand times, if the result is the same in our case." This was confusion of thought on Jack's part. But what better could

be expected? For Rose, with her gentle graceful manner, gave him both her hands, and said—
"Mr. Westcombe, I will think kindly of you."

The bloom of a bright blush deepened on her
cheeks, as her eyes met his courageously; and
then she turned her face away, lest any tell-tale
tears should own, that her promise had been
fulfilled already.

"I will ask no more," John Westcombe said,
longing to see her face again, but like a man,
forbearing; "you have given me all that I can
expect. There are many obstacles between us.
But as sure as I love you, they shall vanish.
Now darling, give me one sweet flower, from
where the sweeter head has been."

A tear fell into her nosegay, as she stooped
to choose a pretty one; and without a word,
she gave him a truss of woodbine, seven sweet
rosy bells.

Then she took up her hat; and trembling
fingers played among the other flowers; because
he might think her sadly stingy, for only giving
him that one.

But it was the one, on which the tear had
fallen, as Jack's sharp eyes had perceived with
joy.

"This flower shall be with me all my

life," he said, as he held it reverently; " now Rose, my Rose, I must see you home; because there are great rogues about. You shall go in front, and I will watch you; as I mean to do all my life."

CHAPTER XV.

AMONG THE CORN.

WHEN big rogues are about, which happens seven days in the week at least, honest men, and women, feel the deepest interest in them. Not from fear alone; oh no, even the women are not afraid; but partly from pure joy at having one's neighbour robbed, and not oneself; and partly from jealousy of beholding enterprise beyond one's own. Any play, that has a fine thief in it, makes us heartily thump the floor; and the tale of his life holds us suspended, until the dear hero is *sus. per coll.*

Any such romantic doings of the night are doubly refreshing to the human system, in the glare of day, and the social glow, and the radiant encouragement of a large beer-can. And when the men have worked hard, and earned their talk, and have women among them, at once to enliven, and chasten, the tenour of their discourse, the truth of their tales receives a flash of fancy, at which they will shudder, when they go home, in the dark.

"Farmer Willum" (as Mr. William Bird was called, to distinguish him from his brother John) was renting, besides his Moorland farm, on which he would never think of trying to grow wheat, a snug little piece, of about thirty acres, down in the lowlands below Christowell. Here there was rich alluvial soil, stolen by the river from its earlier stage, and spread out well above the reach of floods, for man to stick his staff of life in. And Farmer Willum had stuck it in well, with stable support, and the increment of cows; ere ever the farmers began to be cheated, with stuff they now test in their tobacco pipes. But not to say a word, that might afford ground of action to any artificial company, it would be a libel to deny, that Farmer Willum had got a very prime piece of wheat just here. He was as proud as Punch, about it, although he only said—"Middling, well middling. I have seen worse, and I have seen better. In these bad times, us must be thankful, for aught that it pleases the Lord to send. But a' never would have been like that, without sixty load of muck, as I drawed in."

Now the day was come for reaping this, after Farmer Willum had been in and felt it, and found the kern gone out of milk, and looked fifty times at his weather-glass, and tapped it with his knuckles, every time, to detect any wavering of its hand, and listened for it to tick—for he never could understand how it could go without ticking; and after a long council with his wife, who despised a clock that never told the time of day, down he went to the *Three Horse-shoes*, on a Saturday night, when all the useful men were there; and he said through a beard, that would be reaped to-morrow,

" Drat the weather; I can't make head or tail of 'un. And John Sage never cometh here now. But rain, hail, or shine, I've a made up my mind, to cut they three Ox-lands, Monday morning. Any of you lads, as has worked for me afore, come into the traveller's room, and speak your minds concerning it."

And now, here they were, and had been hard at it, up to eleven o'clock of day, according to the stroke from the high church-tower, which came down the valley, and rejoiced their hearts.

Then they flung down their sickles, and they

left their binds; and the children, who had long been endangering their spotty fat legs, among the flash of steel, raced down to the ditch, for their father's knotted kerchiefs, or hats, according as the case might be, and brought them with a dutiful sniff at the contents, to the spot where the cider-barrel stood upon its wheels.

The sun was very strong, and it was time to call a halt. Brawny men wiped their reeking brows, and untied the fillet, that kept their shaggy hair back; and some, with stiff legs bowed by straddling, went down to the brook, to cool arms and faces. The rest made straightway for the cider-barrel, where Mrs. Willum sat upon a milking stool, to temper liberality with justice. And this was a thing requiring care, and quick memory, as well as strength of mind; so many were the tricks of crafty men, coming with a hat on, coming with it off, coming with their neighbour's hat, meanly sending their neighbour's wife, when their own had had it; and worst of all, turning their coat, like liberals, for the sake of another pint out of the spigot. But the farmer's wife was tolerably sharp; and the sharpest of them cheated her no more than twice; and that was the stupid Sam Slowbury.

For this was a man of such deliberation, and so many children, that a very distant gaze was needed, to take a sinister view of him. His countenance alone, and his style of thinking—which could be seen in his forehead when he did it—and the gentle kindling of his eyes, when he began to begin to understand a thing; and above all, the slow and steadfast wrinkles of his smile, which came like a summer ground-swell, as soon as it was impossible for him not to understand—these, and many other gifts, to be envied rather than imitated, proved, beyond doubt, that if nature can be trusted, Sam was the last man she intended for a rogue.

It is not within the present limit, to enter into, far less to settle—as every one does to his own content—points of extreme, and extremely vague delicacy. But for the sake of human nature (which in spite of its own convictions, does not always know exactly what it is about) it is only fair to say, that if Sam Slowbury was a rogue at all, he was so, without privity of his own conscience, and purely for the sake of his family.

" Missus," he said, when he had done some of his dinner, but kept some more to be done yet, and a horn of cider to go after it; "if 'e can foind to spare a minute, come, and zit upon this here stook, out o' the zin; and tell up a bit."

Betty Sage—for Sam was speaking, with this freedom of address, to no less a person—looked at Sam, as much to say, "Young man, you are making too bold, with your betters." But it came to her mind, that the harvest-field might level, for the moment, even the distinction, between the head-gardener of a colonel, and a mere captain's understrapper: therefore she smiled, as Sam showed his horn of cider, and letting down her linsy-woolsy, followed to hear what this labourer might have to tell her.

Slowbury's wits were at their best, because he had been working hard, being compelled to keep pace with the rest, unless he were prepared to taste reaping-hook; and the movement of his body had worked his mind up. Moreover, he was conscious of some cash in pocket; and his consciousness was brisker to rejoice therein, than his conscience to grieve over it. And who shall blame the parent of so many small bread-baskets?

"Why, Sam! I never knowed 'e looked so peart," Mrs. Sage began, almost before they had settled their quarters, upon the two stooks, in a corner the sun had done with; "whativer hath come to 'e now, Sam Slowbury? Too much zider, I reckon—hand me over. I han't had a drop, to count on."

But this solution of his "psychical phenomena," by a disinterested observer, was not satisfactory to Sam. "Naw, naw," said he; "pl'aize to baide a bit. The time of the women-volk beginneth, when the time of the men be zatisfied."

To illustrate this, he sloped his horn, displaying a throat, well adapted for its duties, and intent upon them now, according to the evidence of a sliding lump in front. This was observed by Betty Sage, with a large and liberal contempt.

"Did 'e drame, thou zany, as I wanted thy zider?" she asked, as Sam laid down the empty horn.

"Your maister be getting on bravely, they tell, over yonner to Ockington," said Slowbury, with his tones refreshed; "I have a'-heered zay, putting wan thing with anither, and allowing of what a' bringeth home on Zinday, faive-and-twenty zhillin' a week, be not a brass farden below the vally!"

"What heed of thaine, Sam Slowbury?" inquired Mrs. Sage, leaning forward on her stook, and with sternly set wrinkles, regarding him ; " 'tis the brains as doeth it ; and if the Lord, in His wisdom, hath not gifted thee with a haverage, He hath made it thy dooty not to grumble."

" And I be not a'-grumbling," answered Sam, humbly fingering his big head; " I be quite zatisfied, with my haverage ; though a' don't vetch their vally, out of harvest time. But I coom here, to do 'e a good turn, Mother Sage ; and all I gets for it, is to foind 'e a-zitting in the zeats of the scornful."

" Not the worst of my henemies can say that of me," Betty Sage answered, with politeness, as Sam began to fill his pipe, with a nod of superior indifference ; " if thou hast aught to say, Sam, say it. Thy moother was a sensible woman, before thee ; and many 's the good turn, I've a'doed her. And her always said ' my son, Sam, will repay thee ? ' Can 'e call to mind the red-brick taybeggin ? "

" Ay, and the lather there was, when I brak 'un ; because her were a marriage-present. So be, Missus, I'll be toord, and tell 'e. Don't 'e let your maister ever goo to Weist-Tor, of a Friday night. He be getting on in years ; but the life of him wur gived to him, for so long as he can count it."

"And why, if you plaize, Sam Slowbury, is John Sage to be denied of going to Weist-Tor, of a Friday night? Hath a' doed any sin, for Old Nick to grab 'un?"

"No more nor the main of us, to my knowledge, Missus. And old John be pretty wull a match for Old Nick, with his General sin, to help 'un. But though a' was a fust-fly wrastler, on a time, and could show a good fall yet, wi' sich a chap as I be; what could a' do, Missus, what could a' do, wi' a score of big men a' top of 'un?"

"A' maight crape out. A' can turn winderful," the old lady answered, with a smile at thinking of some of her husband's stories; "but who be they, that he be bound to ware of?"

"I've a' told 'e enough," Master Slowbury answered, shaking all the sheaves of the stook, as he got up. "Rippers be to wark agin; time for me to vall in, or vorvet dreppence."

"Reckon, thou wilt spake agin bumbai. Us shall have to wait upon 'e, zupper-time."

"Missus, it goo'th agin my conscience; and nort but old times wud a' made me zay the words as I have zed. Dont 'e tell no one. For good now, don't 'e."

"I'll pay the dreppence, Sam, for half-an-hour of thee. For good now, stop a bit, and unfold thy maning."

"If I wor to spake anither word," said Slowbury, buckling up his breeches' strap, to go to work again; "twud be worse than the procading of thic beastie, by the gate."

Farmer Willum's donkey had come down the hill, with a basket of refreshment for Mistress Willum, and the maids of the farm, who were hungry; and perceiving no sign of the like for himself, was unburdening his grievances in a loud hee-haw. "You get along, I don't attach no importance to 'e," Mrs. Sage exclaimed, as Sam strode away, with his rip-hoop swinging; "thy moother were a fule, before thee; and I doubt, whether thou be bigger fule, or rogue, Sam Slowbury."

Although her mind was eased by this discharge, in a minute or two, it became again uneasy, as she saw Sam swaying in the reaper's rank. He was the biggest man there, save one, and he seemed to make the cleanest sweep of all; and he laughed, beyond the power of the rest, at jokes, without taking any pains to make his own; the which is the wisest of all human wit.

Betty Sage watched him, and went reasoning with herself, that he must have something in him, to behave like that. And when the reapers halted, in the bottom by the hedge, and one of them sought counsel of Sam, and he scolded a fellow of some cleverness, for setting the stooks up badly, Mrs. Sage was glad indeed, to see Betty Cork come up the rigs.

"I hope I see you well, ma'am. How hot the sun be! But her maketh no difference to your complexion. Ah, Mrs. Cork, with my John away so, I can hardly pronoonce the words inside me."

Mrs. Cork, who was the mother of Solomon (now earning his keep and £5 a year, under my lady at Touchwood Park), and herself kept the chief shop in Christowell, was not come to work, of course, but to look at the work, and deliver her opinion, and jot down the names of the men who were earning corn-wages, and must be looked up next Saturday night, to pay their debts, ere ever they spent them. But though Mrs. Cork had an eye to business, as every one must have to live thereby, she was not above enjoyment of herself sometimes, and of pleasurable doings around her.

Moreover, Mrs. Sage paid ready money, though she might have had credit up to thirty shillings, if she booked her orders; and Mrs. Cork, being of liberal mind, refused to be irritated by the lies, that came to her shop, about old John spending all the loose of his money at Ockington. Her faith in him was, that he kept it all tight, and could not even bear to run a bill up; because of the pain accumulating, at the time of settlement. These meditations made Mrs. Cork, although with her holiday gown on, speak quite as if Betty Sage were her equal.

"And I hope, I see you well, ma'am, also," she replied, with an elegant nod of her bonnet; "if you are as good as your looks, Mrs. Sage, we never need tremble about 'e. 'Tis the sperrit as keepeth our heads up, ma'am; and I wish I wur like 'e; sometimes that I do. 'Tis a down-hearted thing to contend, as I do, without ever a husband, to go on at. He hath been in churchyard, seven year now; and though he took his pleasure ill-convenient sometimes; when it cometh to the slating work, I do miss 'un sadly. What a gift a' had of the rathmetick!"

A person scant of reverence for his betters (when gone beyond expostulation) might have been low enough almost to say, that the late

Mr. Cork's arithmetical gifts were mainly exerted, in doubling the objects within his field of vision. But Mrs. Sage knew what mankind is, and never blamed any man, seven years too late.

"His gifts of discoorse led 'un into faine society," she replied, as she made a soft place for Mrs. Cork; "I've a' often feared the same of my good man; but John sticketh fast by his airnings. I have heered say, ma'am, that your Master Cork could hold his own, with the best of they, as writes this papper!"

"He were the front of them, the foremost on the rank;" Mr. Cork's widow made answer, as she struck a celebrated journal with her knuckles; "I've a zeed him, many times, correct they printers, though a' never zeed a printer's press himzell! Winderful to my mind, however a' could contraive it! I takes in the papper still, for the sake of my Harry; but a' never zim'th to be worth rading now. Half the long words is gone, since they lost his vaine larnin'! Here's a bit of stuff! To think what Harry would a' made of it!"

Mrs. Cork, although she talked like this, was proud enough, as everybody knew inside the shop, of taking, and managing to make out mainly, an admirable journal of the West of England; which combined all the dash of the brightest London style, with a sharpness of wit, which is not to be got, where nobody knows his next-door neighbour.

And now she had brought this paper, not only to jot down upon it the names of her debtors, but also to astound any wide-eared friend, with an article in it, concerning Christowell. "You put on your specks, ma'am, and read that," she said.

This was not a nice thing, for her to say; but rather in the sarcastic vein of the paper she indulged in. For she knew, that no specks of the very highest power would enable Mrs. Sage to make out a single word. "Deary me! I've a been and left my specks at home," said the old lady, after a sham search among her pockets; "but you do read so bootiful, ma'am; would you plaize put your tongue to it, for me?"

Mrs. Cork smiled, because she loved her education; and then, without even putting any glasses on, which made the feat more wonderful, to any one who heard her—which half a dozen women, and a man, began to do—she read, with such disdain of all difficulties, that she skipped them, the following remarkable paragraphs :

"When a matter is beyond our explanation, we have always considered it the most judicious plan, to abide in our patience, until the inexplicable gradually brings about its own solution. With a certain exalted prelate, exalted above the highest scope of human reason, we have felt ourselves driven to adopt this system, because he was amenable to no other."

"Why they've got three column agin' the poor bishop, in this very papper!" Mrs. Cork stopped to say, with a breath of surprise, which proved that she did not understand the sweet manners of journalists; "but perhaps the man who wrote this, forgot all about it."

"But though"—continued this eloquent writer, "we have lapsed into the silence of despair, concerning a ' churchman,' as he loves to style himself, who is all church, and no man; we did indulge a hope, that in our peaceful county, there was nobody else we need shudder to mention. Far, very far, be it from us to institute a parallel, however well suggested, between his lordship of Exeter, and a poor man who has not had his advantages, any more than his sinecure to batten on.

"This poor man appears to be comparatively honest, and to have some very charitable feelings, such as we would gladly find elsewhere. When driven by straitened circumstances to commit a robbery, he does it like a man, and with a tenderness for women, which might afford a lesson to our admirable b——p. And, unless we are misinformed, a certain amount of good feeling characterizes this felon, which has not yet been found, though with many tears sought for, in the precincts of our venerable pile.

"But not to overpress this extraordinary analogy—for we hear that his lordship did weep last week, when he lost a fine appointment for a member of his family—our duty is simply to point out, that measures are about to be applied to this minor Dartmoor evil, which a vigorous Government should rather have exerted upon the more *crying evil* we have feebly indicated. We are informed, upon the very best authority, that as those noble dunderheads, our great J.P.'s, only wring their fat hands, when they can spare them from their knives, and forks, and bottles of old port, at the lawless proceedings of the *unmitred* felon, a very famous general, with a name suggestive of tinder, has been ordered to encamp over against him. We have one great warrior already, in the West, qualified for the commission of the peace, by wholesale slaughter of French patriots; but the remnant of his energies has been absorbed, in the production of grouse, and some other French game.

"We can assure our readers, that we shall observe, with deepest interest, the result of this twofold experiment, this attempt to kill two birds with one stone; premising only two things—that if the poor outlaw could have limited his appetite to farmer's produce, instead of devouring the sumptuous dinner of a Sybarite high-church rector, he might have enjoyed the fine mountain air, for many years, unmolested. Also that, in our very humble opinion, that British commander, of the fire-eating name, might have received more appropriate instructions—to bombard the P——ce of our fire-eating b——p. We trust, that when he has caught the inferior felon, he may gird up his loins, to the larger, more glorious, and infinitely more needful task."

All the good people, who heard this read (as

it was read by Betty Cork, with many sagacious nods at the words that went beyond three syllables), said, "thank you, ma'am; you have dooed it winderful; and winderful faine thic writing be!"

So fine indeed was it—though rather below, than above, this paper's standard—that none of the listeners could make out any more, than that the writer was a clever man as need be, but unfit to have any faith laid in him, without his right name to the foot of it. The rule, to their minds, was that any honest man could get on, with speaking simple. If he wanted to be clever, let him speak it with his voice; there was no such thing, as to laugh by ink and paper; you might as well try to get salvation, from a sermon you clapped eyes upon the parson with his pen at.

But Mrs. Sage was of keener intelligence; as the wife of the seer of the parish should be. She took in a great deal of the meaning of the paper; and added thereto a great quantity of her own. By this double process, her mind became most active, combining conception, and generation.

"Never you tell me," she screamed to Mrs. Cork (who was off, amid a rounder of "Thank 'e, ma'am; thank 'e; plaize to come again, and tell us more;"), "never you tell me that the holy gentleman, with window-blind sleeves, who hath laid his hand dree times upon my head, and bettered me continual, be put alongside of a shape-staling villain, by the biggest thief, as ever wrat upside down. I'd scratt 'un, if I coom acrass 'un, that I wud. and gie 'un the tail of 's own talk."

END OF VOL. II.

LONDON: PRINTED BY WILLIAM CLOWES AND SONS, LIMITED,
STAMFORD STREET AND CHARING CROSS.